D1736237

BOOK 16

CRAIG HALLORAN

Dragon Wars: Bedlam - Book 16

By Craig Halloran

★★★★★

Copyright © 2021 by Craig Halloran

Amazon Edition

TWO-TEN BOOK PRESS

PO Box 4215, Charleston, WV 25364

ISBN Paperback: 979-8-726754-64-2

ISBN Hardback: 978-1-946218-98-8

www.craighalloran.com

Publisher's Note

This book is a work of fiction. Names, characters, places, and incidents either are the product of the author's imagination or are used fictitiously, and any resemblance to actual persons, living or dead, events, or locales is entirely coincidental.

 Created with Vellum

CHAPTER 1—THE PRESENT: WIZARD WATCH

COMMANDER COVIS SAT on one of the pewter thrones inside the Time Mural chamber, sucking grease from his sausage-sized fingers. He gnawed on a turkey leg, tearing the meat off with his gray teeth, and belched.

Gossamer and Datris exchanged uncomfortable glances. They stood side by side, peering into the field of precious gemstones bedded in the Pedestal of Power. The beautiful stones captured the torchlight and shone like bright eyes.

"Try this," Gossamer said, handing Datris a handful of emeralds, and pointed at vacant spots in the field. He was making small talk. After Gossamer had spent grueling weeks putting the pedestal he'd destroyed back together, his plans were put on hold when Honzur the Necromancer and Commander Covis arrived.

Datris carefully inserted the stones into the gaps one by one.

Commander Covis shifted in his seat and started to rise. He swiped his stringy, greasy hair out of his eyes. His dragon armor, crafted from the finest steel in Gapoli, was uniquely quiet. He set aside his turkey bone, wiped his greasy palms on a napkin, picked up a wide-mouthed goblet of wine, and walked down the stairs of the dais. The ape of a man quietly made his way to the pedestal. Towering above the elves, he stood between them. "You make progress?"

Gossamer pushed up his black-and-white robe sleeves and said, "Er... some but far from mastery. The pedestal channels energy from the tower. We're trying to provide a link to it."

"Wizards," Commander Covis scoffed in a rugged voice. His broad face had strong features, hard lines, and dark circles under his eyes. His stare was as hard as iron, and he had a restless nature about him. He took a long drink and set the goblet down on the edge of the pedestal. "How long will it take?"

Gossamer swallowed the lump in his throat. "Well, not long, we hope. It is imperative we galvanize the tower connection. Any misstep could destroy all of us."

"I see." Commander Covis's meaty hand swallowed up the head of the goblet. He lifted it and started to squeeze until his knuckles turned white. "Black Frost wants a quick result. A functional result." The goblet's metal started to collapse in his grip. "I'm here to see it through. Or it's my neck and both of yours." Using both hands, he bent the goblet, crushing it into a little ball. Red wine squeezed out of it and dripped like blood onto the pedestal. "But I'll probably break your neck first before he swallows you whole." He offered them both a threatening gaze. "I want out of this tower. The sooner you make it happen, the better."

"Uh, as you wish," Gossamer said politely with a bow.

"Good." Commander Covis gave Datris the metal ball then dropped his heavy hands on both of their shoulders and squeezed. "You've restored my faith. Don't let me down." He strode back to the dais, walked up the steps, and resumed his seat on the throne.

Gossamer had his back to the Risker, but he could clearly hear the man pouring another goblet of wine and eating his turkey leg. He raised his eyebrows at Datris, who stood with his mouth half-open, gaping at the ball of metal. He returned a helpless look to Gossamer.

Their plan wasn't simple. Over ten years ago, Gossamer had received a visit from Grey Cloak and Zanna Paydark. They'd been sent back from the future, by Gossamer, to tell him what he needed to do when his time came. They were able to fill him in with as much detail as they could, and it had worked, all the way up to the point when he sent Grey Cloak and Dyphestive into the sanctuary of the past. With

Datris, he'd had to replace Zanna's statue in Dark Mountain, reopen the Time Mural, and safely send Zanna Paydark into the past to save Grey Cloak. The plan had gone smoothly, unnoticed, under Black Frost's snout. Gossamer had thought he had it all under control. In fact, he had, until Honzur and Covis arrived.

His thoughts raced. *Black Frost must not trust me, or they wouldn't have come.*

Under Honzur's watchful gaze, he continued his tedious work but carefully took his time about it. If Honzur learned how to use the Time Mural, there wouldn't be any need for Gossamer anymore. With no more Gossamer, the plan would fail.

He took a breath and resumed his work, arranging another pattern in stones.

The slab that sealed them inside the chamber lifted, and Honzur entered. The older wizard was as bald as an eagle. His probing eyes bulged, and the hem of his old wizard robes flapped when he walked. He joined Commander Covis, taking a seat in the other empty throne. The rings on his fingers clacked against the metal arms.

"Any progress since I've been gone?" Honzur asked. He sounded like he was in pain. His voice was hard and biting, matching the ugly scar on his face and burn marks on his arms. "For your sakes, I hope so."

"I believe we have galvanized the link to the tower. It will be time to test it soon."

Commander Covis sat up in his chair. "This is new information. Why didn't you share it with me moments ago?"

"It just happened."

"He plays games, Honzur!" Commander Covis said. "I asked only moments before your return."

"Easy, Covis," Honzur said. "A wizard's craft is filled with many unique checks and balances. So long as we are progressing—"

"Don't patronize me!" Commander Covis stood. "I am a natural-born Risker. Wizardry courses through my veins. Never talk to me like a child that doesn't understand your ways."

Without batting an eyelash, Honzur coldly replied, "Understood, Commander. I should have known better."

"You mock me?"

"I would never do such a thing. Please, join me for a drink. I have a feeling our task nears its end."

A bottle of wine and a goblet rose in the air. Wine poured into the goblet, which floated over to Commander Covis and hovered before his eyes.

Commander Covis slapped the goblet out of the air. He stood up and poked a finger in Honzur's unflinching face. "Dare not test me again, wizard. It will be your last." He stormed out of the chamber, and the slab dropped down and sealed the opening.

Gossamer grinned. *They bicker. Perfect.*

2

GOSSAMER AND DATRIS spent the next few days with the vulture-like Honzur nearby. The elder wizard had a faint raspy wheeze when he wasn't speaking. Often standing in close proximity to the pedestal, he moved little, but his eyes moved much, soaking in every detail of the pedestal.

Datris crouched underneath the pedestal, checking the gemstones that outlined the base. "They are all secure. I've checked every one twice."

"You're sure?" Gossamer asked.

"Of course he's sure. He said he checked it twice, did he not?" Honzur reached under the pedestal and pulled Datris up by the pointed tip of his ear and eyed him. "Or do you need to check it a third time? Perhaps a fourth or fifth?"

Datris shook his head.

Honzur turned his hard eyes on Gossamer. "Enough delays." He tapped his finger on the pedestal. "The time has come to open the Time Mural. Is the pedestal connected to the tower?"

Gossamer nodded. All of his subtle delaying tactics had come to an end. The dragons had come home to roost. "We're ready," he said, trying not to sound defeated. "The tower is linked to the pedestal, but I cannot guarantee the outcome in the Time Mural."

Honzur's gaze fell upon the stones. "Marvelous. I'm eager to see what happens."

"Well, get on with it, then!" Commander Covis pounded his fist on his throne. "The sooner this mission is completed, the sooner I can ride the skies and slay again."

Four large citrine gemstones anchored the corners inside the bowl of the pedestal. Gossamer pushed them down into the bowl one at a time. They sank, clicked into place, and glowed with the light of a campfire. The pedestal hummed.

"The tower and pedestal are connected," he said, catching a concerned look from Datris.

With his decorated fingers and burned, tattooed hands caressing the pedestal's edge, Honzur closed his eyes, tilted his head back, and said in a seductive voice, "Yes, I can feel it. Raw power. Pure and clean." He licked his pale lips. "I've never tasted the likes of it before."

Gossamer felt it, too, every bit of it. Energy seeped

through his skin and awakened the magic nesting in the marrow of his bones. The hairs on the nape of his neck stood up, and goose bumps broke out over his arms.

Commander Covis's armor creaked. He rose from his seat and asked, "It is done, then?"

"Don't be foolish," Honzur replied. "The real journey has just begun." His glassy eyes shone like stars. His fingers dusted over the bright and beautiful gemstones. "Open the gateway," he said to Gossamer.

"But there are thousands of combinations."

"Open the one that was opened last!" Honzur demanded.

Commander Covis's sword scraped out of its sheath, and Gossamer's throat tightened. He'd seen the patterns in the stones before. The underlings had used them, and so had he and Tatiana. He nodded. "As you command."

"Do it," Honzur said.

He began arranging the stones in a precise order, moving his hands purposefully and carefully. "The Time Mural has limitations. It draws on the strength of the towers that are tapped into the mystic veins of this world."

"I fully understand how magic works, fool!" The ring on the middle finger of Honzur's right hand burned, and he stuck it in Gossamers face. "Don't make me burn your eyes out. Open the portal!"

Gossamer moved his hands away from the bowl and leaned back. The large gemstones mounted in the stone archway came to life with a colorful fire of their own. They twinkled, pulsating like a heartbeat. The slab of stone inside the archway started to fade and was soon replaced by the black field of space.

Honzur gasped, stepped down to the floor, and stood before the archway. "It's beautiful. Show me more."

CHAPTER 3—THE PAST: LITTLETON

INSIDE THE WARM walls of a busy country tavern, Dyphestive dunked his buttery biscuit into a deep bowl of gravy, put it in his mouth, and practically swallowed it whole. "Mmm. This was a fine idea, but you know Zanna is going to make us pay for it."

"She can't make it any worse than she already has." Grey Cloak gently sawed off a piece of baked ham. He jabbed it with his fork, added some green beans, and plowed the fork through a pile of mashed potatoes. "Besides, we deserve a full plate of food."

"Don't you mean plates?" Dyphestive raised an eyebrow and lifted his muscular arm.

A serving girl in a white blouse and a long blue dress hurried over. She had big, beautiful blue eyes. Bowing, she eagerly took Dyphestive's plate. "I'll bring another right away, master."

"Er, no need to call me master."

"So sorry. I don't mean to offend." She rushed away.

"I think she likes you," Grey Cloak said.

"I don't know. Perhaps she's jittery. We make people jittery, you know."

Grey Cloak drank from his goblet. "Not me. You, perhaps. Look at you. You look like an ogre in your chair."

"I don't look like an ogre." Dyphestive peered at his arms and hands. "Do I?"

"With this dim lighting," he said, looking at the poorly crafted candle chandelier hanging overhead, "it's hard to tell."

After the harrowing plight at the Rupture and the Temple Ruins, Grey Cloak and Dyphestive had spent years in isolation with Zanna. She'd finally convinced them it was too dangerous to walk abroad. Finally, they'd obeyed and lain low. But that dam wouldn't hold forever.

Dyphestive looked over his shoulder at the entrance.

"Will you stop doing that?"

"What?"

"You know what. Checking for Zanna. If she shows up, she shows up. Make the most of it in the meantime."

"Well, I don't want to make her mad... again."

"Trust me. We are well beyond that point. Drink, eat,

and enjoy." Grey Cloak leaned back on two chair legs. He nodded at the serving girl, who was giggling and smiling among a group of others. "Enjoy your new admirer."

Dyphestive huddled over the table. "Stop saying things like that."

"Why? We are men now. Man up. Be nice to the young lady." He waved at her with his fingers. "She's fetching and reeks of country charm."

"I don't see you flirting."

"Eh, not my sort of folk. I like my women a little more sophisticated."

Dyphestive drank from his jug and wiped his mouth on his forearm. "You don't know what you're talking about."

"No, but you'll fit in well here."

Littleton was a peaceful country community surrounded by leagues of wheat fields and full of hard-working men and women who didn't mind sweating under the sun and enjoyed a hot meal among company after a long day's work.

The serving girl slid another pile of food under Dyphestive's nose. "I brought you some extra biscuits. You seem to enjoy them." She set a jug down on the table. "And here is more milk."

Steam rose from the plate of food, and Dyphestive glanced between it and the woman. "Thank you. You know what I like."

"If you need anything at all"—she brushed against him —"I'll be around. I'm Marilynn."

Dyphestive blushed as he watched her walk away.

"Well, now, look at that," Grey Cloak said. "Your cheeks are as rosy as the wine. You did feel something, didn't you?"

"What are you talking about?" He started buttering a biscuit.

Grey Cloak dropped his chair legs back to the floor. "You were flirting with *Marilynn*. A good thing. Makes you feel alive again, doesn't it?"

Dyphestive's expression soured. "No. It's depressing."

"Pardon? How so? The young gal is splendid."

"I can't help but think that none of them will last if we don't stop Black Frost."

Grey Cloak frowned. "Don't spoil the mood. Enjoy yourself. Eat. No one is urging you to start a family. Be nice to the young woman. With Zanna around, you might not ever get that chance again."

"You're right." Dyphestive dunked another biscuit. Gravy dripped from the fluffy golden-brown delight. He took a deep breath and ate. "Mmm. I love food."

The people of Littleton had hearty appetites and attitudes. In many cases, they wore dirty and dust-covered clothes. Their skin was brown from the sun, and the older ones had deep creases in their faces. They hunched over tables and slopped food into their mouths but carried a happy energy about them, completely oblivious to the dark cloud looming over them.

Zooks. Now Dyphestive has me thinking.

Skreee!

Everyone fell silent. Dishes crashed to the floor. White eyes widened. A portly woman crawled underneath a table.

A farmer burst through the tavern's front door, clutching his crumpled hat to his chest. "Dragons!" he said. "The skies are filled with them!"

Grey Cloak was the first person to slink out of the room and depart through the front door.

Skreee!

Skreee!

Skreee!

Dusk had settled over Littleton. Drakes circled in the sky. Unlike dragons, they were smaller than middlings, with only back legs and taloned hands on the ends of their wings.

Earsplitting shrieks sent the townsfolk running while covering their ears.

Roaaar!

A two-headed grand dragon as black as night dropped down from the clouds and landed in the middle of the town square. Its ebony scales were highlighted with bright-yellow ones.

Two Riskers in full armor climbed down from a double saddle on the dragon's back, removed their helmets, and slung them on the ground at the dragon's feet. They were full-blooded orcs with coarse black hair cut short. After pointing at the tavern, they marched straight toward it.

Grey Cloak hurried back and met Dyphestive at the entrance "We should go."

Seeing the people cowering, Dyphestive said, "We aren't going anywhere."

4

GREY CLOAK MADE his way into the tavern. "Let's see how this plays out, then. After all, they couldn't be looking for us, could they?"

"I don't see how."

They returned to their table.

Grey Cloak picked up his goblet and said, "There was a score of drakes out there, and the Riskers flew on a two-headed grand dragon."

"Two-headed?" Dyphestive asked. "I don't remember seeing many of those in the dragon kennels. Rare, indeed. So, you didn't recognize them?"

"Orcs. Full-blood. Can't say that I recall seeing them in Dark Mountain. I wonder what they're doing here."

"We'll find out soon enough. But if they know us, we might have a problem on our hands."

Grey Cloak smirked. "That will make for two problems. One with Zanna and the other with them."

Men and women gathered at the bay window and stared outside from behind the curtain.

"They're coming this way," one man said.

Chair legs scraped over the wooden floor. Several patrons left coins on the table and shuffled toward the back door.

Marilynn slipped behind Dyphestive and hip-bumped his shoulder. "Don't be alarmed. The Bedlam Brothers will come but be gone soon. They drop in every few weeks or so. We feed them like kings, keep our mouths shut, and pray they move on." She refilled Dyphestive's drink with a trembling hand. "But don't make eye contact with them. It didn't turn out well for the last man who did."

"What happened?" Grey Cloak asked.

"I'd rather not say." Marilynn squeezed Dyphestive's arm. "You might want to cover up. Your brawn will draw attention."

"Certainly." Dyphestive grabbed his cloak off of the chair and put it on. "Thanks, Marilynn. Be careful."

She took a deep breath. "I will."

"Aw, look at you and Marilynn, connecting. She's fond of you," Grey Cloak teased.

"Will you stop with that? Don't the Bedlam Brothers sound familiar?"

Grey Cloak picked at his plate with his fork. "No." He scratched his chin. "I don't think so."

A handful of remaining patrons scurried away from the window and dropped into their seats, hunched over their plates.

The tavern door swung open and banged against the wall.

One at a time, the Bedlam Brothers entered. Their short black hair stood on end. Their hard eyes, as black as coal, swept over the room. Black dragon armor protected their sturdy frames. Swords and daggers hung from their wide hips. They were older, seasoned men, built like bulls, and had broad noses and nostrils that flared. One brother had a curly black beard, and the other was shaved clean. Platinum hoops hung from their pointed ears.

Head down, Grey Cloak kept his eyes averted, but he could still see them out of the corner of his eye.

I've never seen them before. But wait. Oh no! I have *heard of them!*

He caught Dyphestive's worried look. His brother clearly also recalled who the Bedlam Brothers were.

The Bedlam Brothers were renowned Riskers—bloodthirsty killers who executed Black Frost's dirty work to perfection. Among their brethren, they were known as the Sky Slayers, who brought back the heads of Sky Riders on the ends of pikes. Towns crumbled in their devastating wake. Citizens were cut down and mutilated.

Grey Cloak noticed the dried bloodstains on the Bedlam Brothers' armor as they walked toward the bar. The planks groaned underneath their spiked boots.

Patrons scooted tables and chairs out of their way. Conversation had halted. Men sat at their tables with their gazes down.

The bearded Bedlam Brother slammed his metal-covered fist on the bar. "Why so quiet?" he asked in a gravelly voice. "Make some noise, people. You sound like the dead."

Embers inside the fireplace made a loud pop. Everyone jumped in their seats.

The Bedlam Brothers tossed their heads back and roared with laughter.

Forks and knives started scraping across metal plates as people dug into their food with shaky hands.

"Master Gorgo and Master Zog, it is a pleasure to see you again," Marilynn said. She stood behind the bar, filling two massive tankards from a barrel of ale. She set them down on the bar with foam sloshing over the rim. "We'll bring out a feast fit for a king immediately."

"We hunger. We thirst. Make it quick," the bearded Master Gorgo said. "Come on, Zog." Carrying the oversized mugs in their large, hairy hands, they moseyed farther into the room and seated themselves by the fire then pulled over extra chairs and propped up their legs.

Zog lifted his long arm, snapped his fingers, and said,

"Music!" He had a battle hammer that he'd set headfirst by the table. It had a long handle and a metal head engraved with runes.

Music started playing, thanks to a halfling quartet of pipers.

"That's a big hammer," Dyphestive said under his breath.

"Yes, and here you are without your weapon," Grey Cloak replied as he gingerly ran his fingers over the Rod of Weapons propped up by a chair.

"It's probably for the better. We won't draw their attention."

Zog pointed at the farmer in the crumpled hat, who was sitting closest to him. "You, man, come here."

The farmer pulled his hat off, gripped it to his chest, and asked, "Me?"

"Don't make me ask again," Zog warned.

With his head down, the farmer shuffled over. He stood with his knees shaking and his Adam's apple rolling up and down.

"I want you to lift my hammer."

"Pardon?" the farmer asked.

"Lift it!"

5

THE YOUNG FARMER wrapped his calloused hands around the battle hammer and heaved it onto his strong shoulders.

"Will you look at that, Gorgo? This man's got a strong back. Lifts my hammer like it's nothing," Zog said.

"It's very heavy," the farmer replied as he switched the weight of the hammer to the other shoulder. "Heavier than it looks."

"Ah, but you handle it well." Zog gave an approving nod. "I bet you could use a hammer like mine on the farm, couldn't you?"

The farmer shrugged. "I could use a wedge and split logs with it."

Gorgo said, "That's a fine idea. Why don't you let him borrow it, brother?" He guzzled down some brew and wiped his mouth. "We'll come back and get it the next time we're back in town."

"Hmm. What do you say, farmer? Would you like to borrow my hammer to help you split wood?" Zog asked.

The farmer stuck out the hammer and said, "I-I appreciate the offer, but it's far too heavy, and I have enough wood split to carry us through the winter."

With his chin jutting out, Zog asked, "What? You don't like my hammer?" He snatched it out of the farmer's much smaller hands. "It's an insult!"

"No, Master, I did not mean to offend." His chin started to quiver. "It's too heavy for me, and I wouldn't want to damage it."

Zog stood and glared down at him. "You think you can hurt my hammer? What is it? Scrap?" He stuck the hammer head under the man's chin. "Perhaps you think its craftsmanship— my father's father's craftsmanship—is poor!"

"No, I swear. It's a beautiful hammer!" the farmer said, his voice cracking. "A glorious hammer. I'm not worthy."

"You aren't worthy!" Zog said. Using his hammer, he shoved the man in the chest.

The farmer lost his footing, crashed through the table behind him, and fell to the ground. Both the table and the food fell on top of him. He started to crawl away.

"Look at that, brother. He still wants to fight," Zog said.

"Here is your first course of food!" Marilynn said as she

hurried over and lowered her platter to the table. She shoved a whole turkey into the middle of the table along with loaves of bread and bowls of steaming-hot stew. "Hopefully, this will whet your appetite."

Zog turned his attention to the table, set his hammer back down, and took a seat. He looked at Marilynn with a hungry gaze and said, "It isn't the only thing that whets my appetite."

Dyphestive bristled. Grey Cloak tried to catch his brother's eye, but when he couldn't, he kicked him in the shin.

His brother glared at him.

Grey Cloak mouthed, "Stop staring."

The last thing they needed was to attract the orcen brothers' attention. Orcs had a knack for obnoxious behavior, and despite being high-minded Riskers, the Bedlam Brothers had proved they weren't any different. Their reputation preceded them, as they were well-known brawlers who fought at the drop of a hat.

"Thanks for the chow." Zog slapped Marilynn on the rear end so hard that she winced and hurried away. "See you on the next trip."

He and Gorgo laughed.

A war started to rage in Dyphestive's eyes.

We need to get out of here. His ears are starting to steam, Grey Cloak thought.

Careful not to draw any attention, he moved a chair

over and blocked Dyphestive's view of the orcs. Then he slowly wagged his finger at his brother. "We're leaving," he said softly.

The normal bustling inside the tavern resumed. The Bedlam Brothers were noisy eaters, but they kept to themselves. The young farmer slunk out of the tavern through the back. The barmaids made their way back into the fold and began serving the patrons again.

With piper music in the background, the prickly atmosphere began to cool.

Marilynn made her way over to Grey Cloak and Dyphestive's table and asked, "Can I get you anything else?"

"No, we'll be leaving, soon," Grey Cloak said.

"Did he hurt you?" Dyphestive asked her.

"Huh? Oh, of course. I'm used to it. Don't worry, sweetie. They'll have their fill and move out. Once they leave, don't be a stranger and come back." She pinched Dyphestive's cheek. "I'd like that."

"Girl!" Zog shouted, nearly shaking the rafters. He lifted his tankard. "More ale! Hurry! This salty food makes me parched!"

"Right away!" Marilynn said as she hurried to the bar.

"He really needs a punch in the mouth," Dyphestive said.

Grey Cloak leaned into his brother's view. "What are you doing? Trying to bite off more than you can chew?"

"I can handle him."

"*Them*. Them and a score of drakes and a two-headed dragon. Don't make me regret taking you out to eat. Zooks. It should be the other way around."

Dyphestive balled his fist. "I bet I could knock him out. One punch."

"What's gotten into you? Did you fall in love that easily again?"

"No, I don't like them."

"I'm certain that no one does. But we have to deal with it. Eat up, and let's go. We'll come back later, like Marilynn said."

Marilynn returned to the orcs' table, struggling to hold two overfilled tankards. The moment she set them down, Zog pulled her into his lap.

"Ah, this is a dish I like much better." Zog wrapped her in his arms and squeezed.

"Ow! You're hurting me!"

"Give me a kiss," Zog said as he puckered up his lips.

She slapped him. "No! Let me go!"

"A feisty one," Gorgo said with a laugh. He chugged down more ale. "Ask her if she has a sister."

6

ZOG AND GORGO started passing Marilynn back and forth. She tried to squirm away, but the strong orcs reeled her back in.

"Come, now. Don't you want to play with us, little woman?" Gorgo asked as he crushed her in his arms. "We won't hurt you."

Grey Cloak watched Dyphestive's jaw muscles clench. "This isn't our affair, brother. It will pass." But the muscles in his own back tightened. "Let me handle this."

"No, I'll handle it." Dyphestive started to rise.

Grey Cloak tilted his chair back and fell to the floor with a *whack*. He gazed up at the orcs, who sat in close proximity. "Hello, lads." He rolled over, kicked the Rod of Weapons then crawled on his hands and knees and picked it up. Inside his cloak's pockets was a deck of cards he fished out. He set the staff aside, stood before the orcs, and asked, "Would you like to see a card trick?"

The Bedlam Brothers offered him cross looks, but the bearded one, Gorgo, let Marilynn go. "Elf, do we look like fools that enjoy silly tricks?"

Acting oblivious to the danger, Grey Cloak said, "Oh, it's not silly. Watch this." He laid down three cards from a deck of Birds faceup. They were an eagle, a crow, and a crane.

He kept spare decks of cards, among many other things, in his pockets and had spent time playing the game with Streak, Dyphestive, and Zanna during their isolation.

"Pick one," Grey Cloak said. "It's really easy. They won't bite."

The clean-shaven Zog looked at him with a wary eye and poked the eagle.

"Perfect."

One by one, Grey Cloak bent the cards longways, shaping them like a bridge. He flipped the crow and crane over and said, "Remember, the eagle is your card. Keep your eye on it." He flipped it facedown.

Gorgo scooted closer and propped his elbows on the table. "I've seen this game. It's a trick. We don't like tricks."

"I've seen it too. He won't trick me. I have the vision of an eagle." Zog snorted. "Better, even."

"No doubt." Grey Cloak started shifting the cards, watching the Bedlam Brothers' intent stares. Then he stopped and said, "Pick *your* card."

"Easy." Zog planted his finger on the card in the middle. "That one."

Grey Cloak flipped the card over. "Well done. It's your eagle."

"Ha!" Zog slapped his knee. "What do I win?"

"Nothing, this round. But if you wish, we can make it a challenge and play for chips."

With a grunt, Zog reached into a silk coin purse attached to his belt and slapped down a gold coin. "Let me see you match it."

"Certainly." Grey Cloak set down a coin of his own.

Gorgo dropped a gold coin onto the table as well. "I'll play."

"I only do one game at a time. Sorry."

Gorgo slammed his fist on the table. The coins and plates bounced and rattled. "You'll play us both!"

"As you wish." Grey Cloak grabbed another coin and matched the wager. He flipped the cards faceup and said, "Pick a bird. Both of you."

Gorgo picked a crow, and Zog stuck with an eagle. Both of the beady-eyed orcs sniggered. The Bedlam Brothers were naturals. Their abilities were enhanced beyond those of an ordinary man. It gave them an edge in everything. Except they didn't know Grey Cloak had the same abilities.

He flipped the cards facedown and began to quickly sort them. The goal wasn't to win—it was to buy time and distract them. He stopped shuffling and said, "Pick your card."

Zog poked a card and said, "This one."

Grey Cloak flipped it over, revealing an eagle. "Well done."

"Ha!" Zog said.

Gorgo planted a finger on his card.

"Go ahead. Turn it over."

The bearded orc flipped over a crane. "*What?*" he roared. "Impossible!"

Zog laughed at his brother. "Bahahaha! You're a blind fool. I could have guessed that one!"

"Do it again!" Gorgo said with his eyes burning like coals. "I pick crow again!"

"You're *eating* crow!" Zog said.

Perfect. Bickering is an ideal distraction.

Grey Cloak glanced over his shoulder and caught Dyphestive's attention. "Get out of here," he mouthed.

His brother nodded.

Turning back to the orcs, Grey Cloak began sorting through the cards. He'd picked up on sleight-of-hand tricks while walking the streets in Monarch City. He and Zora had played cards a lot back then. Those days seemed like ages ago. He pictured Zora's pretty little face.

I miss her.

"Stop shuffling!" Gorgo said.

Grey Cloak dropped the last card and lifted his hand. "As you wish. Pick one."

Gorgo flipped the one in the middle, revealing the crow. "Ha-ha! I win!"

Zog flipped his card, revealing a crane. "No!"

Grey Cloak turned the last card over, revealing the eagle. "You lose. I win. Shall we play again?"

"Do it!" Zog said.

"Aye!" Gorgo agreed.

Grey Cloak set up hand after hand. He had full control. He let them win some, and for others, he made them lose. He kept them enthralled by keeping the betting even.

Zog finished his ale, wiped his mouth, and leaned back in his chair. Balancing on the back legs of the chair, he lifted his tankard. "Girl! More ale!" His eyes grew big, then his caterpillar eyebrows met. A deep crease split like a V on his forehead. "You! Get away from my woman!"

Grey Cloak turned. Instead of escaping, Dyphestive had remained seated at the table, and Marilynn was sitting on his lap.

Has he gone mad? Zooks!

7

Zog rose from the chair and made his way toward Dyphestive's table.

Grey Cloak moved into the orc's path and said, "Please, Zog, listen to me. I believe there's been a simple misunderstanding." He placed his hands on the orc's chest plate.

The orc marched on, shoving Grey Cloak backward into the table.

"My friend isn't the brightest," Grey Cloak continued. "Marilynn, his fiancée, isn't the sharpest blade in the drawer either."

Zog grabbed him by his cloak's collar, lifted him off of his toes, and said, "Do you think Zog cares, elf?" He slung Grey Cloak aside as if he were made of hay and pointed at Dyphestive. "You! Get away from the girl!"

"No," Dyphestive said flatly.

Marilynn clung to Dyphestive and said, "You don't have to do this for me."

"I think he needs to learn some manners. Clear the table." Dyphestive eyed Zog. "Have a seat."

Zog spat. "I'll break you in two, farm boy."

"We'll see about that." Dyphestive shed his cloak, revealing his muscular arms and shoulders. "How about a simple wager?"

Zog's eyes flashed. "Look at this, Gorgo. A farmer with backbone. I like it. I'll break it."

"There's always a fool in every lot," Gorgo fired back. "Take his bet. I want to see this."

Grey Cloak slipped over to Dyphestive and spoke in his ear. "Are you out of your skull? I told you to leave."

Not taking his eyes off of Zog, Dyphestive replied, "If I leave, they keep coming back."

"This isn't our affair. Don't make this fire back on me."

"Too late."

Zog planted his fists on the table and asked, "What do you have in mind, farmer?"

"A simple contest." Dyphestive stretched his arm over the table. "My strength against yours."

"Pah! Do you hear this, brother? This man believes he can best me. Me! The strongest orc of them all!" Zog boasted.

Gorgo dragged a chair over, sat down, and clawed his

fingers through his beard. "The human's voice does not tremble. I like it."

"Oh, it will tremble when I finish him." Zog sat. "What wager do you have in mind, fool?"

"If I win, you leave and never return," Dyphestive replied.

Zog let out a rusty chuckle. "And if I win, what do you have to offer me? The girl? Ha! You have nothing I need, farmer. I'm a Risker. A valued servant of Black Frost. Your spoils are nothing but rot to me." He put his bulging arm on the table. "When I win, I'll take your woman and your head."

"So long as you agree to leave."

Gorgo's gaze slid between both Dyphestive and Zog. "I like his confidence. Be wary, brother. He might have a snake up his sleeve."

Dyphestive gave them both a cold, dead stare and said, "If you'll notice, I don't wear any sleeves."

Grey Cloak asked, "May I have a moment to confer with my brother? I believe love has blinded his poor senses. We don't want to trifle with the likes of you. Not now, not ever."

"No!" Zog said. "I accept the terms. Gorgo, lock our hands." His lip curled. "When this is over, I'm going to break him apart."

Grey Cloak leaned down to his brother's ear. "You need to walk away from this."

"It's too late now."

Dyphestive and Zog locked hands. Their biceps bulged like ripe melons. Zog was a hairy beast of a man, and his arm swelled underneath the links of his armor. Dyphestive's bare arm—smooth and clean—seemed smaller by comparison but was still herculean.

Gorgo stood and braced his hands over the combatants. He eyed Grey Cloak and said, "Bring candles, elf."

Grey Cloak hurried to the other tables and snatched up the candles that burned on flat plates. He knew where to place them because he'd seen strength contests before. Men would bend their wrists down over the flames, burning the skin on the back of the hand. He placed them in the proper spots.

"The contest begins on my command," Gorgo said. "Don't lose, brother. I like this spit."

With his eyes locked on Dyphestive, Zog said, "You know better than to doubt me. I'll break his arm off and beat him with it."

"I'm counting on it. Go!"

Zog put hard orcen muscle into his push before the *O* in *go* was finished.

Dyphestive matched his stretch, bending an inch at first then pushing back.

The strength in Zog's arm was like that of ten orcs. His

grip was mighty, squeezing like a vise and forcing Dyphestive's wrist back, but Dyphestive held on.

"Impressive!" a wide-eyed Gorgo said. "I didn't think he'd last this long."

"He won't last much longer," Zog growled.

With their free hands, Dyphestive and Zog gripped the edges of the small table.

Dyphestive put his shoulder into it and knitted his eyebrows. The muscles in his face clenched.

Zog fought to lock his wrist backward. He bent it back and pushed. "Hurk!"

They were matched strength for strength. Their locked hands were in an upright position.

"He matches you, brother!" Gorgo said. He slapped his hands on the table. "You embarrass yourself! You embarrass me!"

"Never!" Zog roared. "No one is stronger than me!" His stormy eyes flashed, and he showed his yellow teeth in an angry grimace. He took a deep breath through his nostrils then let out a breath and put his full force into his arm and screamed, "Arrrgh!"

Dyphestive's arm gave. It descended a quarter of the way down, inches from the flame. The fine hairs on the back of his hand started to burn, and the air began to stink. He'd never faced such raw strength before. Zog was a brute —a true powerhouse. He was winning, and the flesh of Dyphestive's hand started to blacken.

8

"THIS ONE DOES NOT CRY OUT!" Gorgo exclaimed. "Remarkable. Zog, you've met your match."

"No man is a match for me!" Puffing, Zog put his full weight into the match. "I will break this human!"

"Never!" Dyphestive said boldly. His skin burned.

With a surge of energy, he shoved back, and Zog's iron strength started to give.

Zog eyed their hands and watched with a horrified expression as Dyphestive pushed his arm upright. His wrist started to bend down. "Who are you?" he gasped.

Dyphestive didn't reply.

"Brother, you humiliate us!" Gorgo pounded his fist on the table. "Push him back! Push him back!"

Zog's hand dipped toward the candle flame. His wooly black hairs started to curl up and smoke. "Argh! No man can match me!" Snorting and puffing, he pushed back with a mighty heave.

The muscles in Dyphestive's forearm swelled. His veins rose and pulsated. He was being pushed back over the top. Hanging onto the wooden table, he put all he had into it. "Ooof!"

Their locked hands teetered back and forth, inching one way and back the other. Zog's wrinkled forehead broke out with sweat.

Dyphestive tasted his own sweat dripping off of his brow.

Zog's boots pushed into the floor. His cheeks turned bloodred then purple. He looked like his head was about to burst.

Dyphestive's arm started to bend backward. "No!" He stomped his foot. "No!" He shoved his hand back to the top and started to push Zog's hand back down.

The tavern broke out in wild shouts and howling cries, though Dyphestive barely heard them through his concentration.

Gorgo got in Zog's face and snarled, "Don't you lose this! You'll be a shame to us all! Beat him, I say! Beat this pink-bellied farm boy!"

The hairs on Zog's hand caught fire. His skin started to stink. His bloodshot eyes locked on Dyphestive's, and he desperately shook his neck. "No man beats me!" He thrust back, bringing his hand toward the top. "No man!"

"I'm not any man. I am Iron Bones!" With a heave, Dyphestive slammed Zog's hand down into the candle. *Wham!*

The small, astonished crowd jumped up, whooping and cheering.

"Silence!" Gorgo hollered. "I'll kill you fools!"

The tavern dwellers scattered like rats and hurried out the door.

Dyphestive rubbed his elbow.

Zog lifted his hand out of the extinguished candle and gave Dyphestive the look of a wounded animal. "You are no ordinary man."

"Neither are you," he replied. "Now, it's time for you to go."

"He cheated!" Gorgo said as he helped his brother rise from his seat. "We will not honor this bet!"

Zog jerked away. "No! This fight is over." He flexed his fingers and massaged the crook of his arm. Slouching a little, he turned his head sideways and said to Dyphestive, "You are a natural. Like us, eh?"

There was no other explanation for Dyphestive's abnormal strength. A natural knew a natural once their gifts were revealed.

He said, "It doesn't make any difference what I am. You lost." He stood. "Honor your word and leave us in peace."

"As you wish, Iron Bones."

The room had cleared out. Only the servants were left,

and they were hiding behind the bar and in the kitchen. Zog returned to his table, bent over, and picked up his hammer. In a defeated manner, he said, "Come, brother. Let us take our leave of this place."

Grey Cloak joined his brother's side and said out of the corner of his mouth, "Very diplomatic and impressive. I didn't see you pulling it off. How do you feel?"

"My arm feels like it's made of lead. I can barely move it. That took everything I had." He watched the Bedlam Brothers quietly confer with each other, muttering angrily.

Zog shoved his embarrassed brother aside again. "Leave me alone! If you're so strong, you arm wrestle him!"

Gorgo gave Dyphestive the once-over. "Pray we don't meet again, Iron Bones. If we catch you out of this farm town, you are through."

Dyphestive started to speak, but Grey Cloak squeezed his arm, so he closed his mouth. There was no sense egging them on, even though his hot blood stirred in his veins. He nodded.

The Bedlam Brothers walked slowly toward the exit. Before they departed, Zog stopped and turned. "Iron Bones. A warrior's name. Not a farmer's." His hard gaze fell upon Marilynn, who stood behind the bar. "Don't waste it making soft babies."

He exited first, followed by Gorgo, and the door slammed shut behind them.

"You did it!' Marilynn ran across the room, jumped into

Dyphestive's arms, and peppered his face with kisses. "We can't thank you enough. *I* can't thank you enough. And to think our modest tavern is still standing. I felt for certain they'd tear it down to the foundation. They did so once before."

"I'm glad I could help."

"You are so strong and so mighty." She rubbed her hand on his chest. "We could bear many strong and beautiful children."

Dyphestive blushed, gently set her down, and said, "I didn't come to start a family. I only wanted to enjoy some hot food."

"Enjoy all you want. Our tavern is yours," Marilynn said happily. "The entire town will celebrate tonight with a great feast." She hurried back into the kitchen.

"I don't think Zanna is going to like this. We might want to beat feet before this celebration gets out of control," Grey Cloak said as he kicked up his rod with his toe. "If we leave now, perhaps Zanna will be a little more forgiving."

"Maybe you're right." Dyphestive wandered toward the exit. "But I'm not going anywhere until I'm certain they leave."

"Yes, well, don't linger. I don't think you did us any favors when you called yourself Iron Bones." He twirled the rod. "What happens if they tell others?"

"Perhaps they'll be too embarrassed." Dyphestive stepped up to the bay window, which had a view of the town's main square. The streets were void of people. There were no signs of the Bedlam Brothers, but their two-headed dragon remained along with many drakes perched on the rooftops. He squinted. "Where'd they go?"

Grey Cloak hurried over. "I don't see them. Something smells rotten."

The floorboards behind them groaned.

Dyphestive and Grey Cloak spun around.

Wooosh!

Zog's flying hammer smote Dyphestive square in the chest with the sound of a thunderclap. *Ka-Pow!* Dyphestive was knocked off of his feet and sent sailing through the window.

9

THE BEDLAM BROTHERS HAD RETURNED. Gorgo's metal gauntlets glowed with the might of wizard fire. Zog's hands were empty, but he gave a crooked, yellow-toothed grin.

Dyphestive lay in the street, unmoving. The hammer flew end over end to return to Zog's awaiting hand.

"You must be Grey Cloak," Gorgo said with fire dancing in his eyes. "We didn't put it together at first, but Iron Bones rang a bell." He massaged his bearded chin. "As I recall, the Doom Riders are looking for both of you."

"The who?" Grey Cloak asked.

"We're finished playing games. Dead or alive, you're coming with us," Zog said as he advanced a step. "Be smart and make it easy."

Perhaps I should have listened to Zanna. What was that lesson she shared about obedience? It's the key to wisdom? After hearing it one hundred times, it's finally sunk in, only a moment too late.

The Bedlam Brothers parted and flanked him.

"There's nowhere to run, elf," Gorgo stated.

The orc was right. Dyphestive's body had already caught the two-headed dragon's attention. It came their way, dragging its long, spiked tail behind it. The drakes perched on the rooftops started to cry.

Skreee!

Skreee!

Skreee!

Zog's cruel snigger was unmistakable. "Huh-huh-huh. I say we smash him. Bust him up the same as his lying, cheating comrade. I want to gnaw on his bones for breakfast." He closed the gap between them.

"Perhaps we can negotiate." Grey Cloak started to slip off his shoes. "You keep your word and leave as you promised, and we won't tell the entire world how my brother embarrassed you in arm wrestling." He raised his eyebrows. "Sound fair?"

"Sounds stupid," Zog stated.

Grey Cloak narrowed his eyes and ignited the head of the Rod of Weapons with wizard fire. "This is your last chance to surrender."

"Pretty," Zog said. The head of his hammer radiated with fire. His brother's metal fists brightened. "But two more can play that game."

Grey Cloak spun the rod behind his back and hunched down. "You had your chance. Now taste the wrath of Grey Cloak!"

Zanna gave the brothers a day. It wouldn't have been the first time they'd run off, particularly Grey Cloak. But they'd been gone far too long, and her head started to pound.

They'd built a comfortable log cabin in the hills. The land had plenty of room to roam and ample vegetation and wildlife, but it was more fit for animals than men. It gave them the isolation they needed to prepare and train.

But it wasn't enough. Boys were boys. Men were men. They wouldn't be tied down forever.

"They should have been back by now." Zanna grabbed her sword belts and sheaths, becoming a woman on a mission. She exited the cabin, closed the door with a bang, and searched for Streak.

The dragon spent much of his time sleeping in a small nearby cave. He only came out to eat or play with the wild animals. He didn't train but watched intently sometimes before slinking away.

Zanna headed up a path behind the cabin to an overlook where Streak could be found basking in the sun sometimes. Nestled in the hills was a cave mouth no taller than her, with its entrance guarded by thorny berry bushes.

Blue birds with red-capped heads scattered out of the bushes as she approached.

She hollered into the cave, "Streak! Streak!"

No response came.

Zanna searched her surroundings, grabbed a nice-sized rock, and chucked it in. "Streak!"

The rock clacked off of something inside.

"All right, already." Streak poked his head out of the cave. "I heard you the first time. Give a dragon a moment to answer." His pink tongue flicked out of his mouth. "Look at you, dressed up to play war."

"Grey Cloak and Dyphestive have been gone longer than a day. They should have returned by now. We need to find them."

Streak yawned, his jaws widening enough to swallow a melon. He eased out of the cave, dragging his belly across the ground and brushing his wings against the sides of the cave. He'd grown a lot over the past few years. He was as big as a middling, sleek but well built.

"A day isn't a very long time," Streak said as he smacked his lips. "Maybe they went fishing."

"I've checked the riverbanks. There is no sign of them. They went to Littleton. I know it."

Streak walked over to the overlook, dragging his twin tails. The two stripes on his back had darkened to pitch-black, and his scales were as gray as stone. He lifted his thick, scaly neck and peered down into the river valley. "A day, you say. You can go a long way in a day. As for me, I can go a super long way." He sniffed. "Do you smell popcorn?"

"What?"

"Never mind. I must have been dreaming about it again." He turned his head back toward Zanna. "So, are we gonna walk, or are we gonna fly?"

10

STREAK DIDN'T TAKE LONG to pick up Grey Cloak's trail. Grey Cloak and Dyphestive weren't being discreet. A blind ranger could have followed Dyphestive's heavy footprints —not to mention that they had both been spotted along the way and had bought a canoe and paddled across the river.

The farther Zanna traveled, the more infuriated she felt. She'd tried to protect them and save them for the future, but they didn't listen.

I'm going to have to take more drastic steps with them.

Zanna and Streak soon gained ground. She'd been right. Grey Cloak and Dyphestive were heading to Littleton. She'd overheard Grey Cloak speaking about it. Zanna and the dragon picked their spots, flying and walking over the land, taking great care for the dragon in particular not to be seen. After a few hours of flying, the wheat fields of Littleton appeared. A small town sat in the middle.

Zanna tapped Streak between his horns. "Take us down. I'll walk from here."

Streak nosedived then pulled up at the last moment, opening his wings, and made a soft landing. "Let me guess. You want me to wait here?"

She petted his face. "You're as smart as you are handsome. Prove me right and wait here while I fetch those two imbeciles." She took off at a brisk walk, arms swinging, fists balled up at her sides.

"Bring them back in one piece." Streak bedded down in the field. "You know where to find me."

Zanna wrapped her cloak around her. Walking into a small town after dusk would draw a lot of attention, the kind she didn't want. She pondered what it would take to fasten Grey Cloak and Dyphestive's feet to the ground. They were young, strong-willed, and eager to live. Keeping them under her watch for several more years would be impossible if she wasn't able to tame them.

There has to be a better way to deal with them.

She'd tried everything she could think of. She gave them the training they needed and worked them both like dogs, trying to break them. But they were young and restless, and she related to that. She'd been the same when she was young, but they needed to be focused.

If I could only get them back inside with the Wizard Watch. I could keep a closer eye on them.

She hurried along the back roads that ran by the barns and cottages surrounding the town. A cluster of buildings no taller than two stories appeared on a western rise. Every shutter and door was closed.

A stench drifted into her nostrils.

Dragons.

Zanna moved behind a storehouse and hunkered down. She spotted the dark silhouettes of birdlike creatures perched on the rooftops and recognized the scaly, bony creatures immediately.

Drakes!

The small breed of dragons were the watchdogs for something bigger—either a firedrake or a full dragon.

It makes perfect sense. Wherever Grey Cloak goes, trouble follows. No wonder this entire town is buttoned up.

She examined the rooftops, spotted several drakes spread throughout the town, and found a path out of their line of sight. Staying low, she dashed from the cover of the storehouse and entered the back side of town.

Skreee!

Zanna froze between buildings. *I hate that sound.*

The dusty streets ran by dozens of shops and other buildings, but there was only one building where the blood brothers would go—a smoke-filled tavern that smelled like baked bread and greasy food.

Follow your nose and keep your ears peeled. You'll probably hear Dyphestive's stomach rumbling.

In the cover of darkness, she moved toward the heart of the town. In the center square, illuminated by lampposts with oil lanterns, a two-headed dragon made its way across the street.

The fine hairs on Zanna's neck stood on end.

Oh no, it can't be.

She spotted a man lying in the street, out cold.

Dyphestive!

Zanna moved onto a porch front. The clamor of snapping wood could be heard inside. Broken glass littered the porch. She tried to peek inside.

Crash!

A figure burst through the tavern's wooden door, skipped off the edge of the porch, and landed near Dyphestive.

She rushed over and kneeled by Grey Cloak.

"Ohhh," he moaned. His face was bleeding. "That hurt." His eyes met Zanna's. "Now I'm really in trouble. I swear it's not my fault this time. Dyphestive did it."

"What happened?"

"We crossed paths with a pair of Riskers," he said.

"I know. The Bedlam Brothers."

"You know them?"

"Everyone with a lick of sense knows them. You need to hide. I'll sort this out."

"But—"

"Shush it!" Zanna put the Scarf of Shadows over his nose. "Go!"

Grey Cloak vanished and said, "I'm not going far."

Zanna lifted her cowl, half covering her face. The hood of her cloak left the rest in shadow. She'd picked it up when she bought supplies from the halflings they bartered with on occasion. She made her way over to Dyphestive and kneeled over him.

Then the Bedlam Brothers exited the building.

Zog smacked his hammer head in his hand and asked, "Where'd he go?" He fixed his gaze on Zanna. "You! Get away from him!"

"I'm only tending to the wounded," she said in a feeble voice. "But I believe he's dead."

"Of course he is. I thunderstruck him. No man can survive that. Clear out, old hag."

The Bedlam Brothers came down the steps, the boards bowing under their mighty frames.

"He's a big one. He'll make a fine meal for Brammom," Gorgo said. The glow in his fists started to dim. "But we must find the other one." He approached Zanna and lifted her by the arm. "You saw the elf. Where is he?"

"He ran. I saw nothing else," she said.

Gorgo slung her to the ground. He whistled for his dragon and said, "Brammom, find that elf."

Brammom lifted both heads toward the moon, opened his massive jaws, and roared.

Drakes returned his cry.

Skreee!

Some dropped down from the roofs and walked the streets while others took to the air, flapping their wings like great bats.

"They'll find him. They always do," Zog said to his brother as Brammom moved away. "In the meantime, we'll make certain his comrade is dead."

11

ZOG NUDGED Dyphestive's arm with the head of his battle hammer then gave him a stiff kick in the ribs. The younger warrior didn't budge. "It hit him square. He should be finished, but his chest still rises and falls."

"Would you expect anything different from a natural?" Gorgo asked.

"I've killed naturals with one blow before. He wouldn't be any different." Zog took a knee, grabbed Dyphestive's chin, and shook his face. "Out cold. He won't wake up anytime soon. Find some cord. We'll bind him up and take him to Black Frost."

"Woman," Gorgo said to Zanna. "Fetch some strong cord. Quickly!"

"As you wish." Zanna scurried away, searching for a general goods store.

At least the Bedlam Brothers' forces were split, giving Zanna the break she needed. The flip side was that the drakes were tearing the town apart searching for Grey Cloak, and terrified citizens were screaming.

She found a general goods shop and spied the owner peeking out of the window. She pecked on the glass. "I need good rope now."

The man had a moustache that connected to his sideburns. He shook his head.

"Either you can give it to me, or the orcs will come and take it. Don't be greedy. You've seen what they can do. What will it be?"

He pointed toward the door and hurried back into the store. The door opened moments later, and he stuck out a coil of rope.

Zanna took it and said, "You made the wise choice." She took her time heading back to the Bedlam Brothers. She wasn't about to let them take Dyphestive or Grey Cloak.

How am I going to get us out of this mess? Buy more time. I'll have to think of something.

Drakes chased a man and a woman down the street. The small dragons burst through doors and crashed through windows, tearing the town apart.

This is madness.

She approached Gorgo and offered him the rope with a shaky hand. "Here is your rope."

Gorgo snatched it out of her hand. "Go away, hag." He snaked out a dagger and started cutting the rope into shorter pieces, then he tossed them to Zog. "Make quick work of it. We need to find the other one and finish this."

"I know how to tie a rope," Zog said as he tested the cord. "But I say we bind him in chains and drop him in a river. Why fool with them? Dead men don't bring trouble."

"The proof is in the porridge." Gorgo glared at Zanna. "What are you still doing here?"

"I was hoping I could keep the extra rope, since I fetched it."

Gorgo tilted his head. "Wait a moment. What happened to your voice?"

Zanna had slipped and spoken in her normal voice. She cleared her throat and answered, "I don't follow."

He grabbed her arm with one hand and pulled her hood down with the other. "You're no hag. You're an elf!" He squeezed her wrist. "What game are you playing?"

"Perhaps she's with them," Zog suggested.

Gorgo peered deep into her eyes. "Why try so hard to hide yourself?" He pulled her cowl down, and his eyes grew to the size of saucers. "Zanna Paydark! You're supposed to be dead!" he exclaimed.

"Hello, Gorgo," she said with a wink. "Have you missed me?"

Dyphestive had played dead long enough. Zog's hammer blow had stunned him, his chest burned, and he could have sworn some of his ribs were broken, but the moment he heard Zanna's admission, he struck.

He opened an eye and closed a fist just as Zog looked away from Zanna and back at him. He slugged the orc square in the jaw. *Whop!*

Zog wobbled and fell flat on his back.

Dyphestive pounced on top of the orc, pinned him down, and rained down punches. "Let's see how you fight without that little hammer of yours!"

The seasoned Zog turned his head aside, tucked in his chin, and blocked Dyphestive's hammering efforts with his arms. His flat nose was broken and bleeding, but he had a snarl on his face. "You're going to have to hit harder than that!" He locked up Dyphestive's arms and spit out a broken tooth. "Farm boy!" He planted his feet in Dyphestive's chest and thrust.

Dyphestive sailed head over heels and crashed into a wagon, breaking it apart. He crawled out of the wreckage and brushed the debris from his shoulders.

Zog stood across the way with his hammer in hand and wearing a wicked grin. "Kiss my hammer, Iron Bones!" He hurled it.

Dyphestive ripped off a wagon wheel and brought it to bear.

The hammer shattered the wheel into pieces, and Dyphestive went sprawling backward.

The hammer's handle wiggled and started to move back toward Zog. Dyphestive dove for it. "It's my hammer now!"

With a cocky expression, Zog beckoned and said, "No, it isn't."

The battle hammer pulled toward Zog with great force, dragging Dyphestive across the ground.

12

ZANNA TWISTED FREE of Gorgo's grip, swept her leg under his, and dropped him flat on his back. Before he could wink an eyelash, she had her short sword at his throat. "What's the matter, Gorgo? You look like you've seen a ghost."

He snarled. "You'll be a ghost soon enough, Zanna!" He smacked her blade aside and rolled to his feet. His gauntlets charged with red energy. "My, won't Black Frost be pleased when I bring him all of your heads."

"You were always a dreamer." She summoned her wizardry and charged her blade with blue wizard fire. "But let's see if you ever learned to dance."

Gorgo charged like a bull and quickly batted her blade aside. Sparks of energy spit off of their weapons. He punched at her face, but she ducked, twisted underneath his swing, and stabbed him in the back of the leg. "You dance as well as ever. Horribly."

"Poke all of the holes in me you want. It won't stop me from breaking your back. Once I get my hands on you, it's over."

"I've heard that before." She lunged and thrust. Her blade punched a hole in his armor, and she skipped back from an uppercut, which whooshed by her face.

That was close.

Zanna pressed the attack. She slashed at his neck, poked at his eyes, and clipped his beard. He parried with hands made of steel.

"You'll have to do better, Zanna. I am a fortress. A mighty weapon. You're too small to best me." He caught her blade in his grip and squeezed tight. "Face my power!" With a jerk, he pulled her forward and socked her in the belly.

She fell to her knees, gasping.

"Perhaps it is you who can no longer dance, Zanna." Gorgo kicked her.

She rolled across the dirt, fighting the pain shooting through her limbs.

Gorgo closed the gap. He kicked her face and sent her sprawling. "And I thought you'd put up a better fight. You look a little feverish. " He picked her up by the clothing and slammed her into a water trough. "This will cool you off permanently."

"Divide and conquer. Not a bad plan, Zanna," Grey Cloak said as he made his way to the outskirts of the town. The clamor of battle could still be heard, and the shrieks of the drakes filled the town.

Brammom crashed through buildings, bursting the timbers like twigs.

I have to do something, or they'll destroy the entire town looking for me. Zooks!

Standing on the edge of town, he lowered the Scarf of Shadows and charged the Rod of Weapons. He waved the glowing head back and forth like a flag. "Looking for me, lizards?" he shouted.

Drakes' long-necked heads whipped around. They shrieked from the ground and in the air.

Skreee!

Grey Cloak started running toward the fields.

The drakes soared, dropped to the ground, and cut him off. In a matter of moments, a score of drakes surrounded him. They spat at him and hissed as their serpentine eyes followed the tip of his weapon.

Roaaar!

Brammom crashed over a storehouse on his way out of the town. He set his four eyes on Grey Cloak and moved toward him. The dragon had huge heads, each with a crown of jagged horns. His eyes were bright white, and milky tortoise patterns were splattered over his dark scales.

"You want a fight? You'll get one." Grey Cloak fed more power into the Rod of Weapons.

Two drakes darted at him as one.

He swung his weapon around and sliced clean through their necks. The heads toppled to the ground.

The rod became a windmill of terror in his hands. Its fiery glow flashed through the air, severing wings and claws, gouging out eyes, and poking bellies. The drakes fell in a dead pile of scales at his feet.

Brammom stormed into the fray. He crushed drakes underneath his girth and released his fire from both heads.

A waterfall of flames poured down on Grey Cloak.

He covered himself in his cloak. *I hope this works.*

Back at Prisoner Island, Thunderbreath's flames had threatened to consume him whole. The Cloak of Legends had saved him then, but he didn't know whether it would protect him again.

The inside of the cloak felt as hot as an oven. Sweat dripped from his nose.

It's hot, but I'm not burning.

The torrent of flames kept coming.

How much flame does this dragon have?

Grey Cloak covered his nose with the Scarf of Shadows as the dragon fire died down. The air around him cooled. He peeked out from under his cloak.

A charred spot smoked around his body.

The flesh of scorched drakes stank.

Brammom's horns tilted from side to side. His large white eyes peered down and seemed to see straight through Grey Cloak. He flexed the talons on his front left paw and stretched it over the spot where Grey Cloak stood.

Zooks!

Grey Cloak rolled to the right as the claw came down on the spot where he'd just been.

The two-headed grand sniffed the dirt and snorted.

This isn't good. Grey Cloak crab walked backward, away from Brammom's sniffing head.

Dragons were like bloodhounds, and Brammom tried to pick up Grey Cloak's scent, continuing to dig up the soft dirt with his claws.

Increasing his distance, Grey Cloak angled back toward town. Moving behind Brammom, he was almost home free, but a drake landed right on top of him and shrieked. *Skreee!*

13

DYPHESTIVE'S LEGS were being dragged over the ground. With both hands, he tightened his grip on the hammer and dug his heels into the dirt, pulling back.

"Let go of my hammer, fool!" Zog yelled. He opened his hand then clenched it again. Then he brought his elbow back, towing Dyphestive and the hammer. "Give it back to me now!"

"Come and take it!"

Naturals had different abilities, and it appeared Zog had a telekinetic connection with his hammer.

Foot by foot, Dyphestive was towed closer to the orc. His thigh muscles bunched, and he dug his heels in, but the packed dirt gave way. He pumped his legs, fighting for footing. Only a few yards separated them.

"Now I have you!" His face was as fierce as a bull's. "Let me have it!"

Dyphestive gave the hammer one last heave.

With a snarl, Zog thrust back.

Dyphestive released his grip, and Zog stumbled backward. His hammer bashed into his skull.

Panting, Dyphestive stood over the bleeding orc and said, "You asked for it." He reached for the hammer.

Zog snaked a dagger out of his boot and plunged it into Dyphestive's calf. "It will take more than a glancing blow to down me!" He snatched the hammer away from Dyphestive's loosened grip and shouted, "Bring the boom!"

Thunder clapped.

The battle hammer's runes heated.

Zog turned his hips into his swing and blasted Dyphestive in the chest. Dyphestive sailed over the busted wagon and crashed through a wall.

Everything in his body hurt. Even his toenails ached, but his chest hurt most of all. It felt like lances had pierced his lungs. He wheezed and spit blood as he tried to crawl across the floor. Grabbing a counter, he started to pull himself up, but his feet slipped, and he fell back down. Lying on his back, he realized he was in the back of a blacksmith shop. Metal tools hung from the ceiling. He stretched his fingers toward the ceiling, where metal poles hung from chains.

"Well, look at who's still breathing." Zog entered the

building through the hole in the wall. He carried his hammer in his right hand and had his left thumb hitched in his girdle. "You must have iron bones in you. Notable."

Fighting for breath, Dyphestive crawled on his elbows, inching closer to a hammer lying on the floor.

Zog kicked it away. "You didn't think that little hammer would do you any good, did you?" He wagged his finger. "Nah, nah, nah. You need a hammer like this." He brought his weapon down on Dyphestive's head and back. *Whack! Whack! Whack!*

Dyphestive broke under his raw power. His body collapsed.

Zog spat and said, "And stay down!"

Submerged in the water trough, with Gorgo's strong hands forcing her under, Zanna summoned her wizardry.

She sent a pulse of energy through her hands and into the walls of the basin.

The wooden seams burst, and the trough collapsed, gallons of water gushing into the street.

Gorgo yanked Zanna up by the hair and said, "Nice trick, but it will take more than that to fool me."

"Is that so?" She sent a charge into her foot and kicked him in the beans.

"Oof!"

The moment Gorgo's grip loosened, Zanna hooked his arm and hip tossed him. Then she kicked him in the head several times. The toe of her boot banged against his hard jaw. "Stay down!"

Gorgo seized one of her ankles and jerked her down.

She kicked him in the face, but his grip held.

"Now I have you where I want you." The orc reeled her in like a fish and grappled with her.

The hard edges of his armor bit into her skin and bruised her bones. She tried to grab a dagger on her thigh, but he blocked it.

"No, you don't."

Gorgo's strength overwhelmed her. He was a mauler and a brawler who'd been crushing skulls for his entire life. His superior strength forced her down, and he pinned her with his legs. "I'm going to bust you up, Zanna." He grabbed her wrist and started to bend it backward.

Zanna clenched her jaw. Agony shot through her wrist. Bone and sinew gave. *Snap.*

"Guh!" she gasped. Her bones had broken. The fire went out of her, and pain took over.

Crossing the Bedlam Brothers was the worst thing they could have done. They were masters of pain and dispensers of destruction. No one they faced ever beat them, not even a single Sky Rider, many of whom had died at their hands.

Gorgo drooled, and he wiped his beard. "Time to surrender, Zanna."

"Not in your wildest dreams."

"You will die, then." The fire in his gauntlets ignited, and he flexed his fingers and brought them down toward her throat. "I'm going to enjoy this."

She wriggled underneath him, but a hard punch to the jaw stifled her efforts and sent her reeling. Bright spots formed in her eyes.

Gorgo was stronger than she was. He was one of the most powerful naturals on Gapoli. Her wizard fire couldn't match his, but she had to try.

Reaching deep, she summoned the mystic energies from the bowels of the earth. Her wizardry pushed against his, forcing his hands back.

"No, no, no." He gave a triumphant grin. "Your strength is no match for mine. None is." His gauntlets came back down, and he closed his fingers around her neck. "You won't be the first, and you won't be the last to die in my grip. Goodbye, Zanna."

Zanna's eyes bulged. His grip was cutting off her air supply. Her windpipe started to cave in. A tear ran down her cheek. Her life flashed before her eyes, and in her final thoughts, she called to her son. *Grey Cloak.*

14

"OF ALL THE MISFORTUNE!" Grey Cloak said.

The drake that had blindly landed on top of him undid the Scarf of Shadows's invisibility.

Grey Cloak punched the Rod of Weapons through its bony chest. "Thanks for nothing!"

Brammom's tail whipped over the ground and knocked Grey Cloak off his feet. He sailed across the ground, skipped a few times, and rolled to a stop.

"Oh, that didn't feel good." He rolled up to a knee and saw Brammom and the drakes charging, both on foot and in flight. "This isn't how I planned my death."

Flames shot out of one of Brammom's heads while the other head struck like a snake.

Grey Cloak dashed away, back toward the wheat fields, but he ran into a barricade of drakes that barred his path.

Like a hive of bees, they attacked, dropping from the sky and tearing into him with sharp claws and razor-sharp teeth. They pinned his arms and tangled his legs.

He gored them with the Rod of Weapons. The bright-blue flare punched through scales and bone.

Clawing and biting, the drakes consumed him, covering him like a colony of bats. Their talons started tearing his exposed flesh to shreds.

"Dragon dung! Get off of me!"

When Brammom roared, the drakes broke off their attack.

Brammom nodded one of his heads to the left and the other to the right. The drakes split apart and gathered beside Grey Cloak in two separate groups.

Eyeing the two-headed dragon, Grey Cloak started to back away.

The grand dragons inhaled deeply. Their chest plates heated, and geysers of flame spewed from their snouts, engulfing the clusters of drakes in fire.

Skreee! Skreee!

The shrieks of the dying monsters reached a crescendo.

Eyes wide, Grey Cloak covered his ears.

Drakes burned and writhed on the grass. Many took flight, flaming wings beating, only to crash to the earth and die.

The shrieking came to an end, and the air quieted.

Brammom stood before Grey Cloak with a hazy look in his white eyes and his necks swaying.

Streak's flat head popped up between the two dragons. He flicked his tongue out of his mouth and said, "And for my next trick…"

Grey Cloak sighed in relief. "Streak! You couldn't have timed your arrival any better."

"Of course not. That's what I do." Streak blew out a ring of smoke. "Wait until you see what I do next."

"The stage is yours."

Grey Cloak.

Zanna's desperate voice entered his mind.

"What's wrong, boss? You look pale."

"Stay put. Zanna's in danger." Grey Cloak dashed toward town, picking up speed with every step.

He cut his way through buildings and rounded the corner to the last spot he'd seen Zanna. She lay on the ground, not moving, with Gorgo sitting on top of her, choking her to death.

"No!"

Grey Cloak charged toward Gorgo, lowered his shoulder, and hit him with the force of a rolling coal cart.

The flattened orc rolled across the road then climbed back up to one knee.

"Mother," Grey Cloak said to Zanna.

She lay lifeless.

"Breathe!"

Gorgo laughed. "What do we have here? Mother and son. How adorable. There's nothing quite like a family reunion at a funeral."

With rod in hand and tears streaming down his face, Grey Cloak said, "You'll die for this."

"What are you going to do? Drown me in your tears?" Gorgo tossed his head back and laughed. "Ha!"

Grey Cloak lowered the rod like a spear and charged.

"Come at me, elf!" Gorgo thumped his chest with his illuminated gauntlets.

At the last moment, Grey Cloak feinted jumping up. Gorgo rose, but Grey Cloak ducked back down, slid under Gorgo's legs, popped up behind him, and rammed the Rod of Weapons through the orc's wide back.

Gorgo flung his arms out and let out an agonized howl.

Grey Cloak ripped the rod out and rushed back over to his mother. He cradled her head in his lap. "Mother! Mother!"

Her neck was bruised with broad finger marks. He put his ear to her mouth, and her soft breath warmed his skin.

He fumbled in his pockets and produced a Vial of Vitality then tore the cork off with his teeth and poured it into her mouth. "Drink, Mother. Drink."

Zanna's eyelids twitched then slowly opened, and her clear gray eyes found Grey Cloak's face. In a raspy voice she asked, "Are you crying?"

He wiped his cheeks. "No. I'm sweating."

"Sure you are. Help me up?" With his arm pushing her back, she rose upright and looked at Gorgo lying face-first on the ground. "Is he dead?"

"It's so hard to tell with naturals," Grey Cloak quipped. "A stubborn lot when it comes to dying."

"I'll say." Zanna stood and stretched like she'd awoken from a long nap. "Where's Dyphestive?"

On the other side of the street, Zog strolled out of the smithy with a bloodstained hammer. His beady eyes fastened on Gorgo. "Blood for blood," he said.

The dark clouds that had gathered started pouring rain, and the streets quickly turned to mud. Lightning flashed followed by a booming thunderclap. *Crack-Boom!*

Zog held his arms up to the sky. Heavy rain washed the blood from his face. "Arise, brother! Arise!"

A bolt of lightning zigzagged down from the clouds, striking Gorgo and emanating a bright flash.

Gorgo's armor glowed red-hot. Rain sizzled on the metal. He rose from the mud with his eyes aglow with white fire. His gaze locked on Zanna and Grey Cloak, and he said, "It's time for one last dance."

15

Holding her broken wrist, Zanna said, "I feared this."

"What happened?" Grey Cloak asked.

"The lightning healed them." She grimaced. "For the longest time, no one understood the unique powers of the Bedlam Brothers, but now we do." She looked up into the pouring rain. "We won't be able to stop them. The storm makes them stronger. We'll have to think of something else."

"I have an idea." He reached for the Figurine of Heroes. "When all else fails, let someone else do the dirty work."

She stayed his hand. "Don't be a fool. You might bring certain destruction upon us. They're slow. We'll use our speed until we think of something."

Thunder clapped. *Crack-boom!*

Lightning rained down from the sky, blasting them off

of their feet.

The Bedlam Brothers laughed.

Grey Cloak rolled his jaw. His ears rang. "I didn't see that coming." He sat up in the mud. "Are you sure you don't want to use the figurine?"

"We're naturals too. We can handle them." She jumped to her feet. Mud and rain slid down her body. With wary eyes, she watched the Bedlam Brothers march toward them. "We have no choice, or we're going to die."

"Quite a speech. I can feel the dirt from my grave already." Grey Cloak aimed his rod at the orcs. "I'll distract them. You go check on my brother." Balls of blue energy shot from the tip of the rod. "Go!"

Zanna ran for the smithy.

The energy balls bounced off the Bedlam Brothers' armor like drops of rain. Grey Cloak turned up the juice.

Zog batted the shots away. "You'll have to do better than that!"

Grey Cloak aimed at their feet, creating a mudhole.

Gorgo stumbled in the hole, tripping his brother.

"Ahahaha! I bet you didn't see that coming," Grey Cloak taunted.

With a scowl, Gorgo climbed back to his feet. "I'm going to make this painful."

"Both of us are," Zog said.

Then Brammom dropped out of the sky and landed on top of them, crushing them underneath his girth.

Grey Cloak couldn't hide his surprise. "I bet you didn't see that coming either. Streak!"

Streak popped up between the dragon's heads and said, "Hey, you left before I showed you my next trick."

"As I said before, the stage is yours."

Streak's eyes brightened like snow. The dragon's heads turned and started breathing fire into each other's faces. Their skulls burst into flames, their eyes burned in their sockets, and scales withered and fell from their necks.

Brammom reared, stumbled on his powerful legs, and toppled. He hit the ground like burning timbers crashing in the forest and splashed down in the mud. *Whump!*

The Bedlam Brothers were still facedown in the sludge.

Streak waddled by the orcs, looking over his wing as he passed them, and said, "Who are they?"

"Trouble."

Streak flicked his tongue. "Should have known, given present company."

Like fallen beasts of the field, the Bedlam Brothers wriggled and fought their way back to their feet. They looked back at their dead dragon with their eyebrows knitted.

The sky filled with thunder, and lightning flashed through the sky.

"They look mad," Streak said.

"Well, they aren't smiling." Grey Cloak climbed onto Streak's back. Lightning came down like hail. "Run!"

Zanna rolled Dyphestive onto his back. "You're as heavy as an anvil." When she placed her hand on his chest, she felt a strong heartbeat. "Thank goodness you're alive."

His face was battered and swollen, and he had huge purple bruises on his back and chest.

"Dyphestive, can you hear me?"

Through a split lip, he said, "That's about the only thing I can do. I think the rest of me is broken."

"I know the feeling."

"No, you don't."

"You're right. I believe you."

Hard rain splattered on the wooden rooftop. Water dripped through spots in the ceiling. Lightning flashed, and thunder followed.

Dyphestive forced himself up to his elbows. "It sounds like war over there."

Since he was a natural, the lacerations on his face had started to mend.

Zanna said, "It looks as if you're going to be okay."

"I always am." With a grunt, he lifted his body from the floor. "Where's Zog?"

"Where do you think?" Zanna stood in his path. "You aren't ready to go out there. They are far too strong in this storm."

"The storm." He punched his fist in his hand. "I'll show them a storm. If I only had a weapon."

"It won't be that easy without a plan." She noticed a wheel from a grinding stone. "And I think I have one."

Zanna carried a small satchel of vials she'd taken from the Wizard Watch. She took one out. "We can't stop them now, but we can defeat them if we splash this on them."

"I'd rather make them eat my fist." Dyphestive snatched the vial out of her grip.

"But don't get it on you."

"I can handle it. Let's go."

Dyphestive led the march out of the room and into a lightning storm.

Bolts of energy came down from above, tearing up the streets and piercing rooftops. Buildings started to burn.

The Bedlam Brothers stood unscathed in their reign of terror.

Dyphestive shouted at Zog. "You!"

Zog looked as if he'd seen a ghost.

"Our fight isn't over yet. It's just begun!"

Zog's face turned into a mask of rage. He raised his hammer high and caught a bolt of lightning. His eyes flickered like fire. The metal in the hammer glowed white-hot, then he gave a battle cry and charged.

16

DYPHESTIVE HALF RAN, half limped toward Zog.

Zog brought his hammer to bear and initiated a sideways strike.

Dyphestive ducked, and the hammer *whooshed* over his head.

After popping the cork off the vial with his thumb, Dyphestive sprang up and splashed the contents in Zog's face then backed away.

"What did you do to me?" Zog wiped a hand down his face and licked his lips. "*Blech*, that tastes awful, and it stings the eyes a bit." But he continued his advance.

"You'll find out soon enough."

Dyphestive was still reeling from the backbreaking beating Zog had given him. It took all he could muster to battle back. His limbs were exhausted, and it hurt to breathe. He clutched his cracked ribs.

Zog's boots splashed through the mud. "Killing you won't come soon enough. This time—" His beady eyes grew as large as saucers, and his legs stiffened. "No! What's happening?"

"A reckoning," Dyphestive said.

The potion's power started in Zog's legs, turning him and everything in his body into stone. It spread to his waist then went up his chest. Armor and skin crackled and thickened.

"You won't get away with this!" Zog said. "Nothing lasts forever." He cast a sad glance Dyphestive's way. "Please, don't do thi—"

Zog's entire body transformed into a perfect statue of a fearful orc warrior holding a great hammer.

Dyphestive planted his hands on his knees and said, "Thank goodness that nightmare is over."

"My brother! What have you done to my brother?" Gorgo cried.

Zanna approached him with another vial of stone and tossed it up and down. "One drop of this, and your days are over, Gorgo. Why don't you make it easy and peacefully surrender?"

He snarled and said, "Surrender is not in my blood. I call the lightning!"

A bolt of energy streaked down from the sky, hitting Zanna square in the back. She sank to her knees, agony spreading all over. The Vial of Stone fell from her fingers and into the mud.

Gorgo pounced, tackling Zanna and forcing her down into the slop. He locked her neck inside his forearm and yanked her back. "This is what happens when you don't die the first time," he said. "You die a more miserable death the second."

Zanna tucked her chin down to her chest, preventing him from getting a full lock. But the pressure built, and her eyes rolled back in her head. The lightning fire searing her body turned on her own inner fire.

"I might die, but I won't die today, you filthy animal!" She summoned her energy and sent a pulse out of her body.

Gorgo went flying and came down flat on his back.

Zanna turned.

Grey Cloak stood over the orc with the muddy vial of stone in his hand. "Looking for this?" He plucked off the cork and poured the contents onto the stunned orc's face. "It once was lost, but now it's found."

Gorgo spat and sputtered, desperately clawing at the air as his body turned to stone.

Streak wandered over to Gorgo and said, "He looks comfortable."

The storm passed, and the night sky cleared. Assisted by several other strong-backed men, Dyphestive and Grey Cloak loaded the statues of Gorgo and Zog onto horse sleds and had them hauled to the Great River. From there, they were loaded onto barges and dumped in the deepest part of the river, never to be seen again.

Marilynn, the barmaid, stayed close to Dyphestive and stood with him at the riverbank, staring out at the moon.

"I can't thank you enough. The entire town is in your debt." She held his hand with both of hers. "No one has ever stood up for me before." She rose on tiptoe, but her lips could barely reach his chin. "Could you lean down so that I can thank you?"

Awkwardly rubbing the back of his head, Dyphestive said, "Oh." He stooped down.

Marilynn kissed him fully.

When she broke it off, she said, "That was much better. Will you stay longer?"

"I wish I could. We'll help you clean up the mess, but it's important that your town buries this battle. Others will come eventually, and the less you know, the better. I hope your people understand."

"Littleton might be a small town, but the people are very close. They understand what's at stake. They hate the Riskers." She kissed his hand and started to walk away. "Please come back and see me again. Goodbye."

Grey Cloak moseyed over to his brother and said, "She was cute. A good fit for you. Maybe you should stay."

"If only I could," Dyphestive replied, looking at Zanna, who was rewrapping the splint on her broken wrist.

"Surely you jest after almost getting us all killed and nearly wiping out an entire town. It's back to the hills, and I pray you both finally understand that," Zanna said. "This battle won't be a secret for long. We have to destroy all of the evidence, including tons of dragon flesh."

"That's one way of looking at it. But consider the other side of the coin. Two Riskers and their dragon are gone," Dyphestive said.

"And that can have an unforeseeable impact on the future." She let out a groan. "You have to understand that."

Grey Cloak put his hand on his brother's shoulder. "We do. And you have *our* word. We won't ever do this again. Right, brother?"

Dyphestive nodded.

"I hope you keep your word this time." She ambled toward them. "Now, let's get back to town. We have to make sure they properly disposed of that dragon."

17

GREY CLOAK, Dyphestive, and Zanna returned to their log cabin in the mountains. The trek home was long, as they traveled with large packs on their backs. Streak and Dyphestive carried the bulk of the load, with Dyphestive towing a sled.

The log cabin wasn't oversized but had plenty of room for all of them. Zanna had the only separate bedroom, and the brothers slept on handmade cots made from stretched animal skins.

"Home again, home again," Grey Cloak said as he sat on the hearth. He tossed some kindling inside and used the wizard fire to ignite it then rubbed his hands in front of the small flames. "Ah, cozy. And we get it all to ourselves for many more years."

Zanna dropped her pack from her shoulders and

sighed. "I've told you. The Wizard Watch is full of amenities."

"Amenities?" Grey Cloak asked with a smirk. "Who needs those when we have the perfect quarters full of nothing."

They'd been going at it most of the way home, hashing over their options. Grey Cloak had made it clear that they would be more careful if they visited other towns and cities. He even offered to use a disguise and swore no one would discover their identities.

"You've done enough damage. We need to lie low for a long while before we even consider it." Zanna sat down on a stool and started taking her boots off. "And the next trip, if there is another, will be under my supervision."

"Fair enough. I'll clam up," he said.

"No, you won't."

"You're probably right, but what else is there to talk about?"

Zanna started unloading items from her pack. "Who says we have to talk?"

"True. We'll sew our mouths shut and make more furniture." He waved a hand.

They'd built every chair, table, and shelf in the cabin by hand. Not to mention that they'd built the cabin from the ground up. The work was hard, but Zanna swore it was a necessary part of their training.

He pointed at a vacant wall. "I think a chair would go well in that corner. I could do some light scroll reading."

"You won't stop, will you?" She set an oil lantern on the table.

"Does it make you want me to leave?"

"Come to think of it, I did enjoy the peace and quiet for a change." She lit the fire, grabbed a few more items from her pack, and headed for the door. "I'll make something to eat. I think you'll like it. I owe you."

"Owe me?"

"Gorgo almost got the best of me. If you hadn't come, I'd be done. Thank you, son."

Grey Cloak's throat tightened. He and his mother had a connection he didn't care to admit. He'd heard her call to him in his head but didn't fully understand it. "I'm sure you'd have pulled through. You're too stubborn to die," he said. "But you're welcome."

She departed, leaving him alone to tend to the fire and gather his thoughts.

Zanna had been right. His selfishness had jeopardized their lives.

I'm getting old. At least twenty seasons. Perhaps it's time I started being a little more responsible. I'll talk to Dyphestive. I'm certain he'll agree. He surveyed the contents of the cabin. The pieces of furniture weren't works of art, but they were as sturdy as tree stumps. *He'll probably be elated. He enjoys the hard work.*

About an hour later, Grey Cloak made his way back outside. Zanna and Dyphestive were gathered by an outdoor cooking pit. Smoke rose from the flames into the star-filled night.

"Something smells good."

Dyphestive wore a goofy smile. "It's the seasoning we brought back from Littleton. It makes all the difference."

"I can see—or smell—that," Grey Cloak replied.

"Zanna says we can build a coop and raise chickens. We'll even get some wild goats and milk them."

Grey Cloak sat down on a flat stone separate from the campfire and said, "I bet you can't wait to get started on that."

"First thing in the morning," Dyphestive replied.

Zanna brought over a metal plate with chicken and eggs and handed it to him.

"Whoa, a knife and fork? We dine like the Monarchs tonight."

"As much as I hate to spoil you, enjoy it," she said then flipped her braid over her shoulder and dug into her food. "At least we don't have to eat with our hands and fingers anymore."

"Or out of Dyphestive's wooden bowls." Grey Cloak sniffed his food. "Mine had a crack in it. So this will do."

Dyphestive joined them. He had a plate twice as big as theirs.

"It looks like your wheel is missing a wagon," Grey Cloak quipped.

"Huh?"

Zanna chuckled.

Streak came down from his dwelling in the higher hills and crept into the camp. His tongue flicked, and he asked, "What's cooking?"

Grey Cloak eyed Dyphestive's full, oversized plate. "'What's left?' is the question. Dyphestive, weren't you supposed to prepare the antelope?"

"Ha-ha. I get it now." Dyphestive ate with his fingers. "Mmm... good."

Streak lay down behind Grey Cloak with his head facing the overlook. "I'll hunt for something in the morning. Getting a little sleepy. Taking over the mind of a dragon, let alone a two-headed one, can be taxing."

In the quiet of night, they enjoyed their ample rations. Even Grey Cloak had to admit that despite the barren surroundings, it was quaint.

I can do this if I have to. I suppose it isn't so bad.

Zanna finished chewing a mouthful of food and had trouble swallowing it. She hit her chest with her fist. "Oh, this reminds me. I brought something special."

She hurried over to the cooking pit, crouched beside it, and returned with a pair of waterskins and metal goblets. "Honey milk. There's nothing better to wash a good meal down."

Dyphestive wiped his arm across his mouth and said, "Perfect. I love honey milk. I didn't know you'd bought it."

"It doesn't keep long, so we'd better enjoy it now. And this is all I have." She drained the first skin into the goblets and handed them over to the brothers.

"Fancy," Grey Cloak said. "And what is the special occasion?"

Dyphestive put his goblet to his lips.

Zanna stopped him. "Not yet. We'll have a toast." She took the other waterskin and filled her goblet. "Raise a glass, men."

They complied.

Zanna stood and continued, "To courage. Strength. Your unfaltering loyalty. The enemies' days are numbered, and our coming days will be short. Be ready. I salute you both."

Grey Cloak and Dyphestive rose from their seats and responded, "Hear! Hear!"

Zanna drained her cup and tossed it aside. "Ahhh!"

Grey Cloak and Dyphestive did the same.

"That was good." Dyphestive eyed the other waterskin. "Can I have more?"

"Certainly," Zanna said.

"Perhaps life on the mountain won't be so bad," Grey Cloak said with a nod. "It's only several years. We can handle it. I might even grow a beard. And perhaps you aren't so bad either, moth—"

He caught Dyphestive's wooden movement.

Dyphestive strained to move his hands, and his body started to transform into stone. "Grey, what is happen—" He turned into a statue with a perplexed look on his face.

Grey Cloak's tongue thickened, and his limbs became as stiff as boards. The last thing he could move was his eyes. They locked on Zanna.

"I'm sorry, son. But you didn't give me a choice. I must protect you." She gave him a sincere sympathetic look. "You both drank the Vial of Stone. Be strong. I swear I'll wake you when the time comes."

No! Grey Cloak screamed in his mind. *Evil betrayer!*

The starlight dimmed, and the sounds of nature became muted. Then his entire existence went black.

Streak pounced on Zanna, pinning her down to the ground, and roared in her face. "What have you done to them?"

"I did what must be done," she admitted with a grimace. "You must believe me, Streak."

His chest scales heated. Smoke steamed from his nostrils. "Grey Cloak was right about you all along. He can't even trust his own mother."

"You saw the disaster they created in Littleton. It nearly killed us all. I had no choice."

"There is always a choice!" he yelled. "Undo what you did, or I'll kill you!"

"It won't last forever. When the time comes, I'll release them. I swear it," she said.

Streak sank his talons into her skin. "You'll undo it now, or I'll rip you to pieces."

"I can't," she said desperately.

He poked her hard in the head with his snout. "What do you mean, you 'can't'? Why would you do something like that that you can't undo?"

"There is a scroll in the Wizard Watch. I need it. It's the only way to undo the spell." She squirmed. "You're hurting me."

"Good."

"Please listen to me, Streak. I know this looks bad, but I wouldn't have risked it if it wasn't safe. And I've been through it myself. They'll survive."

Streak looked over his shoulder at the statues of the Blood Brothers and said, "Are they in pain?"

"No. But it's the worst kind of torment."

Streak got back in her face. "All the more reason to free them now. Get on my back. We're going to the Wizard Watch, and you will fix this."

"Both of us can't go. You have to stay back and guard them until I return. It's the only way to keep them safe. I'll go. I promise—when I return, I'll free them. Please, let me up."

Streak eased off. "You'd better return soon."

Zanna retrieved the Cloak of Legends and the Rod of Weapons.

He cut off her path. "Where do you think you're taking that?"

"It will be dangerous. I'll need all the help I can get."

Streak snapped his jaws in her face. "You'd better not be lying to me. I'll hunt you down, and that will be the end of you. I swear it."

"I'll return." She touched his face, but he shrugged away. "I'm sorry, Streak."

"Save it for them. But I doubt they'll be as understanding as I am."

Zanna headed down to the base of the mountain with tears in her eyes. She had no intention of returning soon. The scroll she needed she had in her possession. She'd planned it all along.

This is the only way.

CHAPTER 18—THE PRESENT: FARSTICK

SOME CALLED Farstick the City of Blackstone. Its buildings were made from dark limestone, giving a shadowy effect, even in the daytime. Unlike the cities in the south, which had rich farmland and green rolling hills, Farstick was a mining town and surrounded by huge rock quarries.

With its back set against the Black Hills of Ugrad, Farstick had thrived and expanded over the centuries. The hills were rich in ore and precious stones as well as coal for burning.

The stone quarries were small cities of their own. Tents had been set up around the rim and down inside as the miners dug deeper.

Dwarven stoneworkers were the taskmasters in the quarries and mines. The stout, hard-eyed, bearded men were covered in grit from head to toe. Ogres worked among them, pushing metal carts filled with rock up the quarry ramps. In other cases, large donkeys pulled them.

The entire area was fascinating but foreboding at the same time. After long hours of work, the citizens could barely manage a smile and mumbled quietly among themselves. One got the feeling it hadn't always been that way. There must have been times when the people were robust and lively. But that had changed.

It only took one quick reminder, and Zora understood why.

Shrieeek!

She shuddered and covered her ears with her hands instinctively, but she brought them back down.

"Hard to get used to, isn't it?" Crane asked. The portly man, who had wavy brown hair, wore his usual friendly smile. His eyes were always warm and playful.

"Even in Raven Cliff, I never became used to it," Zora said as she adjusted her cloak and retied the strings on the neck. "They would wake me up every night after the invasion. A decade of them screaming day and night. Rattling your bones in your skin."

"Doesn't bother me at all," Crane stated. "I used to be married. Talk about shrieking. Oh my. Just thinking about her makes my ears ring."

She gave him a funny look and started to ask about his past but thought the better of it. Once she got Crane started talking, it was difficult to get him to stop. Zora needed to keep him focused.

"Crane, we've been walking awhile. Are we getting close?"

He stopped, rubbed his saggy jaw, looked up and down both sides of the road, and said, "It's hard to say. They keep making the signs smaller and smaller. And I can understand why." He towed her by the arm into the alley.

A quartet of Black Guard soldiers on horseback trotted by. The moment anyone heard the distinct sound of hooves on stone and the jangle of armor, everyone—man, dwarf, orc, or ogre—moved out of their way. Unlike the cities in the south, the people of Farstick were far less robust. They acted more like slaves than people thriving under Black Frost's watch.

Zora eyed the soldiers and muttered, "I hate them."

The forces of Black Frost consumed everything in their path. The Black Guard were thicker than thieves manning the streets. Middling dragons soared overhead. The citizens hurried along from place to place, and often, little children screamed.

"Let's keep moving. A sign will appear. It always does." Crane hurried along after the Black Guard had passed. He waddled a little when he walked but moved at a brisk place.

Zora followed.

She eyed the tall, ominous buildings. Farstick was vast, bigger than Raven Cliff but smaller than Monarch City. It was one of the largest cities she'd been to. Some buildings stood four or five stories tall. Towers of tribute over ten stories tall were the centerpieces of grand gardens. Everywhere she went, it felt like the walls were closing in, and every window was watching her.

"This is what it's going to be, isn't it?" Zora asked, catching up with Crane.

He gave her a perplexed look. "What do you mean?"

"In the south, the forces of Black Frost are chummy. Reeling in the Monarchy and dangling golden carrots before the citizens," she replied, gazing about. "But this is what it's really going to be like, isn't it? Or worse?"

Crane clasped her hand with his warm one. "Only if we don't stop it. Come on. I think I've spotted something."

A middling dragon soared above them.

Shrieeek!

Zora flinched and said, "I hope so."

Crane hustled over to the entrance of a general goods store. A small potted plant with tiger lilies sat on the edge of the stoop. He subtly pointed at the plant and winked at Zora. "That's our sign."

She hadn't noticed any flowers in the dreary city before, and if Crane hadn't pointed them out, she wouldn't have noticed them at all. She followed him inside the store.

Customary of most general stores, it had a little bit of everything one would need. On the floor were wooden barrels filled with wheat, barley, beans, and flour. Blankets, shirts, and trousers were stacked up on tables. Dresses hung on racks. Tall wooden shelves loaded with goods of all sorts lined the walls from floor to ceiling.

Two halflings approached Crane and Zora. One sat on the other's shoulders, so that they were roughly the same height as Crane and Zora. They were men and wore long cotton shirts with sleeves rolled up to the elbows and trousers held up by suspenders. They were very businesslike, aside from their bare feet.

"Can we help you?" they asked in unison. "A new cloak, perhaps? Or perfume for the beautiful lady?" They raised their eyebrows. "We have dresses too." They opened her cloak. "Perfect for your lovely figure."

Zora brushed the seemingly harmless little men aside and said, "That won't be necessary."

Crane lifted a cotton smock with a sunrise pattern, his mouth opened in an *O*. He gasped and said, "I love this. Do you have one a little bigger?" He held the shirt to his chest and smoothed it over his belly. "I'll look good in this."

"Of course we have your size. We have every size, from halfling to ogre," the halflings said. "Don't go anywhere. We'll be right back." They hurried away.

"Crane, what are you doing? We aren't here for clothing." She eyed the smock. "And that looks awful."

He frowned. "Oh, you think so? I think it brings out my eyes."

Zora took the smock out of his hand and said, "I don't

think it will matter so much what you're wearing once we're behind the Flaming Fence."

"I can't help it if I want to look good no matter where I go."

She blew a strand of hair out of her eyes and crossed her arms. Crane's unflappable personality gave her little comfort in the gloomy city. She wanted to leave, but she had even less desire to seek the Dragon Helm behind the Flaming Fence. However, it had to be done. "Let's get this over with."

The halflings appeared from behind a curtain that led into a back room and waved them back.

Crane waggled his eyebrows, smiled, and said, "The brotherhood knows we're here."

19

REGINALD the Razor lifted a spoonful of light-gray porridge and let it drop in clumps back into the bowl. "Quite a place Crane found for us to wait. It looks like something Tatiana would cook."

"It's not bad," Sergeant Tinison stated. The wooly haired, loud-mouthed honor guard from Monarch City was shoveling the porridge in. "I've had worse in the field. And it was green. Was never sure what it was. I swear that stuff moved." He winked. "Right inside and straight out."

"Yes, well, it's not for me. I'll try something else." Razor pushed the bowl back and waved a hand at an orcen barmaid with a lot of meat on her bones.

She shooed him off with her napkin.

"I don't guess I'm being given much of a choice."

Talon had gathered on the edge of Farstick in a run-down tavern called the Greasy Pit. Moth-eaten curtains hung in the window that had a view of the street. The walls were grimy and gray, and the floor didn't appear to have been mopped since it had first been put down. The rafters were full of cobwebs, where spiders with bright-red bodies and white spots fed on insects. The floorboards creaked, and the smell of tobacco smoke and burnt food hung in the air.

Aside from Razor, Tinison, Gorva, Beak, and Tatiana, only a few people were inside the tavern, including the one-eyed man tending the bar and the orcen servant woman. Their personalities were as stony as their appearances, and they didn't talk much.

Tatiana sat closest to the window, staring outside. The sorceress wore her long, silky hair in a topknot, and her elven features were strong and gorgeous.

"You should eat," Beak said next to her. Also known as Shannon, she was the daughter of the fallen Monarch Knight Adanadel and had joined with Crane and Tinison to help bail out Zora and Bowbreaker back in Doverun. She was a strong, well-built warrior with refined mannerisms and a former member of the Honor Guard.

Gorva, an orcen natural and a warrior's warrior, sat with her back to the fireplace, eyes closed and arms crossed.

Tatiana turned from the window view and said, "Apologies. I can't help but think I should have gone with them."

Razor dunked a hard piece of bread into his bowl of

porridge. "Zora and Crane know what they're doing. But I'm all for finding another spot to wait."

The orcen serving woman took his bowl of porridge away.

"Say, put that—" He caught her intense glare and said, "Never you mind. I'll be fine drinking this delectable wine while enjoying what's left of this crunchy bread."

"I like the crunchy bread. It reminds me of my mother. She used to burn everything," Tinison said. "You should eat, Tatiana." He eyeballed her plate. "But if you aren't going to, I'll be glad to finish it for you."

"Help yourself," Tatiana said softly as she turned her gaze back outside.

Razor leaned over the table and asked, "Is there something going on we're missing, Tatiana? You're being very distant."

She shook her head. "No, but in truth, my mind races. We've never embarked on a quest like this before. The Flaming Fence is the most dangerous place in the world."

"Maybe it won't be so horrible. It wouldn't surprise me if it offered better food than this."

Razor dropped his bread on the floor, and a mangy little dog that sat by the hearth hurried over. It trembled like a leaf, grabbed the bread, and slunk away.

"That's one big rat."

"I have faith in us," Beak said. She lifted her wooden mug. "A toast."

Everyone sheepishly lifted their mugs.

Beak sat up proudly and said, "To do what is right. Strength to our limbs. Steel in our backs. Minds as sharp as razors. Long live the Monarchy!"

"Hear! Hear!" they all said. "Hear! Hear!"

"Thank you. I feel better now," Tatiana said with her eyes watering.

"What's wrong?" Beak asked.

"You remind me of your father, Adanadel. I spent many years with him. A stalwart and honorable warrior." Tatiana dabbed her eyes with a cloth napkin. "His time ended far too soon."

Beak scooted closer. "Tell me more about him. I only spent most of my time with him when I was a little girl. I remember his sunny smile and handsome face, but he was also so stern and dedicated."

"He lived the life of a true Monarch Knight. If he knew what became of them, he'd be ashamed." Tatiana scooted closer and rested her arms on the table. "When Dalsay and I were asked to lead the quest to retrieve the dragon charms, we knew we needed to search for warriors who believed in our cause. The talk of Dark Mountain ruling over the world was considered lunacy back then. So many laughed in our faces, unable to see the coming darkness.

"But Adanadel believed. His pure heart allowed him to see through the veil of deceit. He felt the presence of evil long before we approached him. He stood ready."

"How did he know?" Beak asked.

"The same way you did. The same way we all did. We have the ability to discern right from wrong. You know it when you see it," Tatiana continued. "We aren't alone in this gift. There are many, but they don't have the courage to act on it. Others allow themselves to be blinded and let the spread of evil, which poses as good, take control." She rubbed her shoulders and stared at the small candle burning in the middle of the table. "If we fail in our mission, then the entire light of the world will be snuffed out. All freedom will be lost, leaving only destruction and darkness."

20

Zora and Crane followed the halflings into the storeroom in the back.

The halflings opened the lid to a metal trunk and said, "Come. Come."

Inside the trunk was a staircase going down into a dark room. One of the halflings climbed in first. Carrying a lit candle, he made it down one flight and waved them forward.

"Are you sure about this?" Zora asked Crane.

"Of course I'm sure. I'll go first." He climbed into the trunk and went down the wooden steps.

Zora followed and met up with the others at the bottom of a narrow corridor that only went one direction.

The other halfling stayed up top, waved his fingers, and closed the lid.

"So good to see you again, Master Crane," the halfling man said.

"You, too, Jasper," he replied.

"Ah, I should have known you knew them."

Crane put his hand on the halfling's shoulder and said, "Yes, this is Jasper, and his brother is Whisper. We go back a good ways."

"I take it you know who we're going to see, then?"

"Not necessarily. It's imperative that our members don't stay in the same place too long. We rotate."

The noises of activity came from above them. Horses and wagons were moving. Zora had the feeling that she, Crane, and Jasper were walking from one side of the street to the other. The tunnel felt much the same as the catacombs below Monarch City, where they'd dealt with the Dark Addler guild and half-man, half-goblin rogue, Irsk Monco.

The corridor dead-ended at a wall of iron bars leading up.

Jasper braced his back against the wall and said, "Everyone join me."

The moment they placed their backs the same way, the wall started to rotate, forcing them to shuffle their feet until they faced the other side. A crudely hollowed out tunnel was held up by wooden rafters and beams.

Jasper grinned. "You thought we were going up, didn't

you?" He winked up at Zora. "There's nothing quite like well-played misdirection."

"Thank goodness. My knees started aching at the thought of climbing up those rungs," Crane said.

"Don't worry, Master Crane. We're close," Jasper said as he took off down the tunnel.

"Why does he call you Master?" Zora asked.

"Because I'm the master of many things," he said cheerfully.

The tunnel sloped downward, and the sound of water trickling met their ears. At the bottom of the tunnel, a shallow, smelly stream joined the tunnel. Zora covered her nose.

Jasper waved them on and said, "It's a little sloppy from here on out, but we don't have to go much farther."

"I have to admit that it's a great place to hide, so long as you can stand the smell. What is that?" she asked.

"Sulfur. You'll get used to it," Crane said.

She shook her head and tried to walk on the edge, keeping her feet out of the water. "No, I won't. And I don't think I'm alone. I haven't seen anything else alive down here but us."

"This way. This way," Jasper said.

Farther down the tunnel was a yellow light. The cool, damp air started to warm.

They entered an alcove, where a small bridge crossed over the stream into another chamber. A broad set of stairs moved up toward the source of light. Torches hung in brackets in the circular room, which had a domed ceiling. The chamber was sparsely furnished but cozy. The floor was covered in exquisite rugs along with fur blankets and pillows on a back section of the wall. A round mahogany table sat in the center of the room, and incense burned in the middle of it.

A lone woman sat at the table with her head down, flipping over cards. She was a lizard woman, attractive in her own way, with silky scales like a snake's and a shapely figure showing underneath her cloth tunic dress.

"It's been a long time, Crane," the lizard woman said in a pleasant voice. Her speech was polished, unlike the raspy voices of lizardmen. She set aside the cards and looked up at them. Her pretty eyes were a pale pink. "You haven't aged a day and are as handsome as ever."

"And you are still gorgeous, Sasha," he said with a bow. "Will you marry me?"

Sasha laughed politely. Her modest stone-and-metal jewelry rattled on her neck and wrists. "Not this again. Perhaps I'll marry you the next time we meet." Her pretty eyes slid over to Zora. "And who is this?"

Crane hooked Zora's arm and led her to the table. "This is a dear friend of mine, Zora."

"Ah, I should have known. Tanlin's pupil." Sasha inspected Zora. "A lovely girl." She extended her hand. "A pleasure to meet you."

Zora shook the lizard woman's hand. To her surprise, Sasha's grip was silky and warm. "You as well."

Sasha offered her hand to Crane. He peppered her with kisses all the way up to the elbow.

She gave a weird hissing laugh then said, "How do you tolerate this lovesick fool?"

Zora shrugged. "One gets used to it."

"Please, join me," Sasha said, indicating the additional chairs.

Jasper reappeared from the shadows, carrying a wooden tray with a jug of wine, silver goblets, a bowl of grapes, and a plate of cheeses.

"So, Crane, I'm curious. What brings you as far north as Farstick?" Sasha batted her eyelashes and squeezed his hand. "It can't be because you missed me."

"Well, of course it is," he said in an exaggerated manner. "I had to ask for your hand at least one more time while the breath is still in me."

Sasha began pouring wine and serving her guests. "Yes, I'm sure that's true, but aside from that, what is it you need?"

Crane rubbed his stubby finger under his lip and said, "We need a guide."

The lizard woman nodded politely and took a drink. "Interesting that *you* need a guide. And what is your destination?"

Crane leaned over the table and said with a smile, "The Flaming Fence."

Sasha gave a belly laugh. "Crane, you always know how to make me chuckle." Then she noticed his and Zora's somber expressions and said, "Oh my, you're serious."

21

"IT'S NOT OFTEN I'm surprised," Sasha said, her painted claws toying with the rim of her goblet. "But here you are, with a bizarre and insane request."

"I know it's a tall order, but it is urgent, and I wouldn't know where to start in the mountains," Crane replied.

Sasha rose from the table and began to circle the room. Her legs were long, and her dress split in the back just above her tail, which dragged behind her. "I'm curious to know what you're seeking."

"The less you know, the better," he said. "But think of it as a rescue mission. I hope that helps."

Sasha nodded, stood behind him, and played with his curly hair. "I can only imagine it has something to do with Black Frost, so I won't pry." She whispered into his ear, "But I could extract more information from you if I wanted."

With a joyful smile, he said, "There's no doubt about that. So, will you help us?"

"It's not a matter of *will* I help you but *can* I help you. That's the question." With her back to them, she put her hands on her hips and sighed. "The Flaming Fence, of all places. Wouldn't you rather take a tour of Dark Mountain instead?"

"We already know the way there. Had a rendezvous with Deeann years back."

"Did you ask her to marry you too?"

"Er, well, maybe..."

Sasha giggled. She rubbed his shoulders and said, "If I didn't know better, I'd think you're crazy, but you've always done what is best for Gapoli. I'll find you help, but as I alluded to, it won't be easy. The trek into those foothills is perilous enough. I believe they put it there for a reason. Even fools wouldn't venture there."

"We aren't fools," Zora interjected. "I don't think there is a name for what we are."

"I like her. She has grit. A true student of Tanlin. Please give him my regards when you see him again."

"I will," Zora said. *If I ever see him again.*

"Crane, as always, it's been a pleasure. I'll need a little time to find someone suitable for your mission. Tell me, where are you staying?"

"The Greasy Horn on the southern edge of town."

"I know the place. I'll send your escort there, but it might take a couple of days."

Crane scooted his chair back, stood, kissed her hand, and nodded. "We'll be waiting."

Zora welcomed the warm sun on her face on an otherwise chilly day after the cramped tunnels underneath the city streets. For a moment, life didn't seem so bad, as the high sun cast away the shadows. All was well until the Black Guard rode by, casting gloom over their shoulders.

"Two days?" she asked. "Isn't that long?"

"You aren't in a hurry, are you?" Crane replied.

"No, I suppose not." She glanced back at the soldiers. "But the farther away from the Black Guard we are, the better. I tire of seeing them."

"Yes, it's a shame. But many of the soldiers don't know any better, and none of them have a choice." Crane strolled down the street and added, "Be glad that we do."

Skreee!

Zora hunched her neck down into her shoulders, glaring into the sky at a dragon that flew by. "I hate that."

"We all do."

Blending in with the crowds of working-class people, they navigated back toward the Greasy Horn using a different route from before.

The hairs on Zora's neck rose. "Do you get the feeling we're being watched?" she asked as they crossed into an alley.

"I always feel that way. It's usually women admiring my manly stature. You'll get used to it," he said, sucking in his belly. "But in a womanly sort of way."

"No, that's not what I mean." She could have sworn she felt eyes on her back. "It's something else. Something familiar." She grabbed his hand and picked up the pace, leading him through the alleyways as if he were a child.

Crane stumbled along the first few paces before gathering his footing. "What are you doing?"

"Shush."

They took one quick turn after another, then she dragged him into the back entrance of a butcher shop. Flies were buzzing over flanks of hanging meat. They ducked behind a small portal window with a view of the alley and peeked out.

"What are we looking for?" Crane whispered.

"I'll know when I see it."

"But I don't see anything."

"I know that. Shush," she said again. "You're like a child. If you weren't so big, I'd think you were a halfling."

"I used to be."

Zora clamped her hand over his mouth. "I don't want to know." She looked through the window for the longest time. Her racing heart beat in her ears, and she couldn't breathe.

"I think you're being overly cautious," Crane said.

"Perhaps." The tension in her back started to ease. "Let's go."

She'd just started to rise when a giant bat-winged eyeball flew by. *Flaming fences! A yonder!*

22

"I DON'T CARE about those buggy yonders, but what I do care about is living in this scat hole another two days," Razor said. He eyed his empty goblet. "The food and drink are awful."

"Quit complaining," Gorva said. "All you do is complain."

"If you don't like it, you can leave. Or better yet, I'll leave." Razor stood.

Zora and Crane had joined Talon in the Greasy Horn and shared their news.

"Please, sit down," Zora said. "Someone knows we're here, and they're watching us. We need to prepare."

Razor sat back down and crossed his arms. "Well, I'm so hungry that I could eat a yonder. It couldn't taste any worse than the porridge we're eating."

"Poor you and your delicate palate," Gorva said with a mocking smile.

"Goy, I have standards. Nothing wrong with that."

"Anyway," Zora continued, "I believe we shed the yonder, but from what I know of them, they'll be looking."

"I wouldn't be overly alarmed. Monarch City was chock-full of yonders. They spooked everybody," Beak said. "It's no surprise they would latch onto you if they haven't seen you before."

"Perhaps you're right, but I don't want to take any chances," Zora said as she removed her satchel and hooked it on the back of her chair. "No one leaves the tavern. We stay low until our guide arrives."

"Fantastic. There's nowhere else I'd rather be," Razor said. He lifted his arm. "Another jug of wine, darlin'. We aren't going anywhere."

"I want to hear more about your conversation with Sasha," Tatiana said.

"Well, she laughed when I told her where we were going. When she realized we were serious, she made it clear it was a suicide mission," Crane stated and sipped a spoonful of hot porridge. "My, this is awful." He shrugged. "But I've had worse."

"What do you think, Zora? Can Sasha be trusted?" Tatiana asked.

Zora replied, "How can anyone know for certain?"

"You have good instincts," Tatiana said. "Better than mine."

"Well, I trust her if Crane does. I sincerely believe she will help."

"Or she could be the one that sent the yonder after you," Tinison interjected.

Crane shook his head. "The Brotherhood of Whispers doesn't operate with those vile things. And I've known Sasha as long as anyone. Everyone, be patient. She'll come through, and when she does, we'll find a way to slip out of here without drawing the attention of the yonders."

"In the meantime, everyone should rest. We'll have a long journey ahead," Zora suggested.

"Listen, I'm not sitting around for two days. I need to stretch my legs." Razor stood. "With your permission."

"I'd rather you didn't," Zora replied.

"I'll go with him," Gorva suggested. "Don't worry. I won't let the child go too far."

Zora nodded. She wasn't entirely comfortable with leading, but they were looking to her, so she tried to not overdo it. "Better you than me."

With a smile, Razor offered Gorva his elbow and said, "A nice day for a stroll. And I knew you couldn't wait to get me alone."

Gorva shoved him in the back. "Get going."

"Ah, it's good to stretch the legs and get out of the stench of that rotting inn," Razor said as he stretched his arms back. "Now, what do you say we get something good to eat? I can smell beef roast from a league away."

They walked side by side through the streets of Farstick with their cloaks on and their hoods down, allowing them to blend in better with the crowds.

"I don't remember you being so impulsive when it came to food," Gorva said. "It's all you talk about."

"Perhaps I'm obsessed with the thought that it might be my last meal."

"You shouldn't think like that."

"Eh, I normally don't, but everything I do seems to matter. And keep this between me and you. I don't want the others to think I'm soft."

"I'm sure that won't happen."

Razor continued, "I'm a young man. All of a sudden, the little things matter. The food, the sun on my face, the smell of freshly cut flowers. I never paid any attention to those things before, but now, I can't get them out of my head."

"You're growing up."

"Is that what this is? It's horrible." He rubbed the stubble on his chin. "Come to think of it, it has been over ten years since I joined Tatiana. It doesn't seem so long."

"My father always warned me that life can catch up with you all at once. Be careful where you step." She nudged him with her shoulder. "Especially when it comes to other people's toes."

"But I'm really good at that. I'll be thirty seasons soon, and I don't have a family. My brothers and sisters have big ones, but I'm the youngest one in the family." He shrugged. "For all I know, they all think I'm dead by now. But the first time I saw a sword, I knew I wanted to be the best sword fighter in the world. So, have you seen any yonders?"

Gorva grabbed him by the wrist and towed him deep into an alley.

"I guess that's a yes."

She pinned his shoulders against the wall and said, "No, I haven't seen any yonders." She pressed up against him.

"What, then?"

Gorva kissed him then broke it off. "Stop talking." She kissed him again fully. "Stop complaining." The next passionate kiss lasted a long time. "You're driving me crazy."

He wrapped his arms around her taut waist and kissed her back like no woman he'd ever kissed before.

With their bodies pressed together, they sank into the shadows of the alley, melting in each other's arms.

When they broke it off, they were both panting. Gorva's chest heaved.

Razor's heart pounded. "I think you found the secret of keeping me quiet."

She managed a laugh, rose to her feet, and said, "Keep this between us, or I'll silence you forever."

With a broad smile, he watched her tantalizing figure walk away. "I knew she liked me."

CHAPTER 23—WIZARD WATCH

THE ARCHWAY of the Time Mural revealed leagues of a hard and bitter land. Vegetation was sparse, and the hills and slopes were covered in scattered rock formations. Two setting suns glared down on the cracked ground. Small dust devils floated across the dusty terrain.

Honzur shielded his eyes. He'd stood in front of the mural for the longest time, staring at the valleys of dead land. "Show me more," he insisted.

Gossamer passed his hand over the Pedestal of Power. Mystic energy surged through his blood. The image in the archway scrolled across the unchanging landscape. Datris stood nearby, watching him carefully.

Commander Covis wandered out of his station on the pewter throne and joined Honzur. "What is this place? It's ugly and bitter."

"It is another world. The one the underlings were summoned from. It's the only pattern in the stones that I remember," Gossamer replied.

"Black Frost wouldn't have use for a place such as this. There is nothing," Covis said.

Honzur twisted the rings on his fingers one by one. "Nothing that we can see." He stretched his hand forward.

"I wouldn't do that," Gossamer warned.

The wizard pulled his scalded fingers back and asked, "How does one cross safely from one world to another?"

Gossamer had plans for that. He hoped to find an opportunity to shove Honzur and Covis into another world, the same as Grey Cloak had done to Dirklen and Magnolia. "I don't think crossing into another world is a problem. The trouble is coming back."

Honzur arched an eyebrow. "Yet this has been done before?"

"Yes, with Tatiana."

"How so?" Honzur asked with his eyes still fixed on the scrolling image.

Datris gave Gossamer a concerned look and small head shake, but Gossamer opted to be honest. "We made her a collar that tethered her to this world and allowed us to summon her back."

"Fascinating. We'll need more collars," Honzur said.

Gossamer and Datris exchanged glances.

"For what?" Commander Covis asked.

"If Black Frost needs a new world to drain, we'll need to take a closer look."

Covis fixated on the image in the mural and asked, "What world is this?"

"I believe the underlings called it Bish," Gossamer answered.

"It looks worthless." Covis turned and walked back to the throne, picking up a jug of wine from the stairs. "I suggest that you find another."

Gossamer nodded.

Honzur shook his head. "No, this will be as good a place to test our abilities as any." He turned to Gossamer. "How long will it take to make a collar such as the one you mentioned?"

"Not long. A few weeks, perhaps."

Honzur narrowed his eyes and said, "That won't do. I want it fashioned in a few days. More than one. We have ample resources in the Wizard Watch. Use them!"

Datris calmly stepped forward and said, "We should not test the mural without consulting Black Frost."

"Is that so?" Honzur replied. "Do you think he'll be satisfied with only a portion of the work completed?"

Datris's calm demeanor turned rigid as he walked down the pedestal dais. "I've worked by Black Frost's side for more than a decade. No one understands his expectations more than I do. He needs to be aware of what is going on."

"That's why I am here," Honzur said. He pushed Datris

back up the stairs with the tips of his fingers. "To keep him aware. To sniff out treachery and disloyalty. You will do as I say."

"But I insist."

With a wave of his hand, Honzur sent Datris flying off of the dais and across the floor. The ring on his middle finger shone an eerie yellow. The horrified Datris skidded across the floor toward the opening at the base of the mural.

"Perhaps you will be the first one to journey to Bish. You can eat the sand and dirt forever."

"Enough!" Gossamer cut off his connection to the Pedestal of Power. The image in the Time Mural faded into a wall of solid stone. "We work together, not against. Datris is Black Frost's overseer. One of his chosen. Raising your hand against him is a criminal offense."

Honzur released his telekinetic hold on Datris and said, "Don't trifle with me, Gossamer. I know my authority, and I am well within my bounds."

"We've seen nothing official from Black Frost. We'll be sure to verify it with him on our return trip. In the meantime, I suggest that we continue to work together." He moved to Datris and helped him back to his feet. "We'll work on the collars immediately. Perhaps you can assist."

"Pah. I didn't come to assist. I came to oversee." Honzur walked to the pedestal and placed his hands on the rim. "I'd stand back if I were you."

"Wait. What are you doing?" Gossamer asked.

Honzur's rings and eyes begin to smolder like fire. Gossamer pulled Datris out of the way.

The portal started to open anew, revealing a huge picture of a barren landscape.

"Ah." Honzur moaned with delight. "I have opened the door, and I like it." He cackled. "I like it very much."

Gossamer had underestimated Honzur. The evil wizard had learned more than he'd bargained for. "Careful, Honzur. You are the link between two worlds. It can drain you."

"Yes, I feel it. But you know what else?" Honzur's face was a mask of evil. "It can fulfill me too."

CHAPTER 24—FARSTICK

"IT'S BEEN THREE DAYS," Zora said to Crane.

They were sitting in a room on the second floor of the Greasy Horn that overlooked the street.

Crane's legs were propped up on a chest at the end of the bed. He sat in a chair, smoking a cigar. "I know, but Sasha will come through. She always does."

Tatiana sat on the small bed with her legs crossed and her eyes closed, meditating.

Meanwhile, Zora stood next to the deteriorating curtain in the open window, staring out. "I don't like this. Ever since I saw the yonder, it's felt like something isn't right."

"You're thinking about it too much. Be patient. Wait. Our situation will reveal itself one way or the other."

She turned and asked, "What do you mean, 'the other'?"

He puffed out a ring of smoke and said, "If something is amiss, it will rear its ugly head. Besides, the waiting game is an important part of the Brotherhood of Whispers. Keep quiet. Allow the information to come to you."

"You make it sound as if we're a part of the brotherhood."

He shrugged. "You might as well be. After all, there isn't an initiation to make it official."

"What do you mean? How do you know you're one of the brotherhood?"

"You're invited. Either you accept the invitation, or you don't." He huffed out several more rings of smoke. "I remember when I was invited. I didn't even have to think about it before I said yes. And the woman who asked me, she was a marvelous creature. Tall and put together like she was sculpted out of pure porcelain."

"What was her name?"

"Oh, I can't tell you that."

"Why? Would you have to kill me?"

He scratched his head with his cigar hand. "No, it's because I can't remember her name. Helga, Florence, Harriet, Eileen, Zora—"

"That's *my* name."

"Oh, that's right, and a fitting name it is." He started muttering more names.

Zora turned her attention back to the street. She'd been

watching through the windows day and night, and her patience had worn thin. She picked her lip.

Skreee!

Startled, Zora pulled off a piece of skin. "Ow! I've had all the dragon calls I can handle for a day. I think I need to take a walk." Her hand instinctively went to the Scarf of Shadows, which was no longer there. She thought of Grey Cloak, and her heart sank.

"It's broad daylight outside," Crane said. "Are you sure you want to do that?"

"I can't sit in here anymore. I have to do something." She buckled her sword belt and grabbed her cloak. "I'll cover up, and I won't be long."

Tatiana opened her eyes. "I should join you. My legs could use a stretch."

"I could massage them for you," Crane offered.

"No, thank you." Tatiana tousled his hair. "But thanks for offering."

Zora opened the door and came face-to-face with Sasha.

Sasha shoved her back into the room, moved toward the window, then closed it and the curtains. The lizard woman's naturally calm and cool demeanor was gone. Her eyes swept through the room before she finally sat on the bed.

"Apologies," Sasha said, "but the task at hand proved a little more difficult than I initially determined."

Crane joined her on the bed. "What happened?"

"You were followed into the store, only a bit later. Whisper kept your pursuers occupied. There were two of them, a man and a woman. Riskers. They didn't make any bones about finding you." Her voice trembled. "Whisper is dead."

Zora gasped. "They killed him?"

"They dragged him out of the store and tortured him. Left him in the store as a warning. Whisper's wounds were extreme. He didn't survive, but he didn't talk," Sasha said with a sob, but there were no tears. "He was a dear friend. We'd been together for decades. Jasper is heartbroken."

Crane hugged her shoulders. "This is my fault. I'm sorry. We should have been more careful."

"We *were* careful," Zora said in disbelief.

"Forgive me for what I'm about to say, but is it possible there is a traitor in your company?" Sasha asked.

"That's unlikely," Tatiana said as if she'd been slapped in the face.

"Beak and Tinison are new to the group," Zora said with her eyes on Crane. "Are you sure you can trust both of them?"

Crane gawped. "I can't think of two better people, present company excluded, of course."

Zora moved to the window and peered down the streets. From all appearances, it was another perfectly normal day. People walked through the streets, pushing vendor carts, and horses and mules pulled wagons. The Black Guard patrols had made their presence known.

"Can you tell us more about the Riskers?" Zora asked.

"Poor Whisper didn't say much. A man and a woman in dragon armor. He mentioned the smell of brimstone." Sasha sat back. "I didn't come to mourn. Whisper died to protect our secret, and it is safe with us. I have procured a trustworthy guide who will meet you in the hills north of the city. I will lead you there, but we should leave immediately."

"Of course," Crane assured Sasha. "I'll round everyone up."

Tatiana introduced herself to Sasha, offered her hand, and said, "I'm sorry about your loss."

While the other women made small talk, Zora examined her thoughts. She and Crane had departed Sasha's lair through another building. A yonder picked up their travels soon after that, and only Sasha and Jasper knew where they were. She eyed Sasha, who was looking at Tatiana. Something gnawed at her stomach. Sasha sounded pretty vague on the details.

Can I trust her?

Crane popped his head back inside the door and asked, "Everyone ready?"

Sasha was the first to stand. "We need to depart quickly."

25

TALON SLIPPED OUT of Farstick on foot, leaving the horses and wagons behind. They moved with small packs of gear on their backs, blending in with the workers who traveled in and out of the city.

Sasha led the trek, walking with fluid purpose while talking with Crane, who struggled to keep the pace.

Trailing behind the others, Zora checked over her shoulder time and again. Increasing the distance between them and Farstick did little to quell her discomfort.

Tatiana fell back from the company and joined Zora. "You appear grim. What's bothering you, sister?"

"It's Sasha. I've been restless since I met her."

With the sun on their faces, they hoofed it up to the first long rise that led to the Black Foothills at the base of the mountain range.

"You trust Crane, don't you?" Tatiana asked.

"Of course, but he can be too trusting at times." Zora's foot slipped on the loose ground, and she grabbed Tatiana's arm. Steadying herself, she said, "I'm not sure why we left our horses either. The ground is awful, and there's plenty of traffic on these roads."

Trains of workers hauling wagons of ore and coal entered the mountains from all directions. Ahead, mining camps were set up at the base.

The mountains had been mined for many ages, and the paths that winded from the hills were rugged. There were deep ruts and overgrowth in the washed-out road.

"I think we're safe," Tatiana said. "We've become a tight-knit group. It's difficult to welcome an outsider. Remember, we were all new once."

Zora nodded. "Yes, I remember, but that was ages ago."

Her eyes found Razor and Gorva. They walked shoulder to shoulder, helping each other on the rocky slides.

"What's going on with them?"

"You noticed too?" Tatiana gave a smile, which she didn't often show. "Perhaps that is what ails you. A little bit of jealousy."

"Did you make a jest? Surely Gapoli is at its end." Zora chuckled. "Believe me. It's not jealousy. After Bowbreaker, well, I think..."

"You think what?"

"I wish him well, but I have to move on, and it won't be with Razor."

"Yes, well, that option might be off the table, unless you want to tangle with Gorva."

Zora gave a quick burst of laughter. Everyone stopped and turned.

She gathered her composure and waved them on. "Don't mind me. I'm fine."

The company resumed their journey toward the Black Foothills of Ugrad.

"Whew. Perhaps a good laugh is all I needed."

"I think you're right. You have been focused on protecting us, a burden of leading that isn't easy."

"Feel free to take the baton from me at any time," Zora offered.

"No, I like it better this way." With a smug smile, Tatiana separated from Zora and resumed her climb behind the others.

"How'd I get myself into this?" Zora muttered.

She picked up the pace and headed to the front, passing Beak and Tinison and giving them a nod. She caught Razor and Gorva's hands brushing against each other, but they quickly split apart.

When Zora caught up with Crane and Sasha, she asked, "How much farther?"

"Once we separate from prying eyes, we'll meet your guide at the base of the Black Foothills. He'll be ready,"

Sasha said. "West is a fine mountaineer. Hence difficult to reach." Sasha jumped over a deep rut and helped Crane over. "No one knows the foothills better than him."

The little bit of information gave Zora some more comfort. She decided to keep Sasha talking.

Staring at the northern horizon, she saw nothing but giant hills waiting to swallow them like ants. Black trees that didn't look like anything Zora had seen before swelled at the base of the mountains. "The foothills are true to their namesake, I see. The leaves are black."

"Yes, the foothills are unique. I've only seen them a few times up close before." Sasha towed Crane behind her. "They are a blanket of dark clouds when you stand beneath them. But the bark burns green, and the leaves have a velvety feeling." She pointed at the gaps in the foothills that created a straightaway into the mountains. "The timber grows quickly, and lumberjacks have to cut them back. A land that does not want unwelcome guests is a difficult land to conquer."

"You make it sound like the mountains have a mind of their own," Zora said.

"They do. One only needs a long conversation with a druid to be convinced."

Crane's chubby cheeks were flushed, and he said in a winded voice, "I don't know how you two can walk and talk so much. I'm out of breath." He gasped. "I think I've been riding in my wagon too long. I need my special boots."

"So, is the entrance to the Flaming Fence hard to find?" Zora asked.

Sasha shrugged. "I know little more than you do. Few have seen it and lived to talk about it. West has been there. So he says."

"So he says?" Zora exclaimed. "You don't know whether he's been there or not?"

"I can only take his word for it, and his word is good. I wouldn't fret. West is as trustworthy as anybody." Sasha lifted her tail, and Crane latched on. "I would be more concerned with getting in and out of the Flaming Fence once you find it. But according to West, that won't be easy either."

"Of course not. Nothing we do ever is," Zora said. "We're used to it."

26

WEST WAS a barrel-chested bear of a man dressed in a long-sleeved shirt made of red wool and forest-green trousers. His full salt-and-pepper beard was unkempt, and his eyes were as cunning as a wolf's. The head of an oversized timber axe rested on his brawny shoulders. The mountain boots he wore laced up above his ankles and had a fur lining. But his most distinct feature was his large ears.

He crushed Zora's hand in his leathery palm. "The Flaming Fence, huh?" His heavy gaze swept over the company. His strong voice had a natural, earthy charm. "I have to admit that I was eager to see what sort would want to undertake such a foolish mission." His fingers clawed through his beard. "Now I know."

Looking up at the mountain man, Zora asked, "Can you take us there?"

"Aye, but I won't take you in." He eyed Sasha. "That's where I draw the line."

"You aren't expected to do anything other than that," Zora said, rubbing the chill from her shoulders.

The trees of the Black Foothills soaked them in shade. The air was cool and damp.

Crane had sat down and taken his boots off. He had red blisters on the sides of his feet. "How much farther to this place?"

"It's a climb. At least two days' journey with good weather." West eyed Crane's feet. "That doesn't look so good. Yer feet will be raw to the bone before we're halfway up the mountain. Not meant for townsfolk."

Crane gave Zora a defeated look.

"Don't worry about it, Crane. Stay with Sasha if you wish," Zora said.

"Well, are we going to stand around and talk all day, or are we going to climb the mountain?" Razor asked. "I'm ready to get this over with."

Skreee!

Skreee!

Beak stood near the edge of the foothills where they'd entered and met with West. "Grand dragons. Two of them!" she said.

Zora and the others joined Beak. The dragons were far away, skimming the ground like seabirds that dove for fish.

"Sasha, do you think those are the ones that were looking for us?" Zora asked.

"I hate to assume anything, but that would be my guess."

Crane's mouth hung agape. "They're coming straight for us."

"Yes, almost as if they knew we were coming." Zora knocked Sasha to the ground and pinned her by the throat with her dagger. "You told them where we'd be! Didn't you?"

Sasha hissed. "At this point, it should be painfully obvious. A shame you didn't figure it out sooner rather than later. You should have trusted your instincts, Zora."

Crane came over with a hurt look in his eyes. "Sasha, why? You've betrayed the brotherhood."

"Fool! I am not Sasha. Sasha is dead." She transformed into a perfect image of Crane. "I am something else far greater!"

Crane gasped. "A changeling."

Zora's skin crawled, but she held her blade firmly against the changeling's neck. "Wink a lash, and you won't be anything."

"Oh, you wouldn't want to hurt yourself, would you?" The changeling transformed into Zora but kept her forked tongue. "Be wise. Surrender. The Riskers only want to know what you seek inside the Flaming Fence. Share that information, and they will spare you."

"They're getting close," Razor warned.

Zora's blood boiled. She had to act. Looking down at her own mocking expression, she said, "We aren't telling you or them anything!"

"Then I'll watch you die while the information is tortured out of another!" Her tongue shot out, coiled around Zora's neck, and squeezed hard.

Zora choked. Fury swelled inside her, and she couldn't contain it any longer. She stabbed the changeling in the heart. A stroke of her other blade clipped the tongue from around her neck. She peeled it off and stared down at the changeling.

The creature's skin was as smooth and white as a snake's belly. It had a head and a face but no distinct features. It lay dead, wearing Sasha's clothing.

Zora pushed up and said, "I'm sorry about your friend, Crane."

"That wasn't my friend."

"No, but I fear the worst for the real Sasha."

Skreee!

"Zora!" Tinison shouted. "We're going to have company at any moment."

"This way! This way!" West said.

"How do we know he isn't one of them?" Zora asked.

"You don't," West said. "But Sasha contacted me three days ago. I've been waiting here ever since. Come with me. I know a place where the dragons can't go." He offered his axe to Zora. "I swear on my axe that I'm as confused about this as you."

"Changelings are rare. The chances of two being in the same place are nearly impossible," Crane said to Zora. "We can go with him, or we can fight the dragons."

"West"—Zora handed him his axe—"lead the way."

"It's going to be a brisk pace. Everybody keep up, because I'm not slowing down to kiss some dragon," West said.

Using the cover of the trees, they raced through the foothills toward the base of the mountain, then they started a steep climb with the rocky terrain slipping under their feet.

Crane fell and slid down the hill. Gorva picked him up, tossed him over her shoulder, and resumed her climb.

Behind them, the roar of dragons carried through the woodland. Branches popped and snapped against their girth. Heavy footsteps were coming.

"West, how far is it? They're closing in!" Zora said.

He pointed up. "We have to make that ridge, then we'll lose them in the mines," he said. "Now stop yapping and climb!"

Zora moved to the back, seeing to it that everyone kept going forward. Everyone scrambled up the steep hill like their feet were on fire. She looked behind her. A bright flash of dragon fire illuminated the forest like a lightning storm.

Roaaar!

The dragons were closer to them than Talon was to the ridge.

Zora started back up the hill just as a dragon head appeared among the trees with its horns lowered.

We're not going to make it.

27

ZORA OPENED her satchel and withdrew her flat, oval-shaped dragon charm. Warm energy surged into her fingertips, flowing down her arm, into her shoulder, and meeting with her mind. She crouched behind the rocks.

The lead dragon swung his head around, and his penetrating gaze met hers. His mouth opened, and smoke blasted through his teeth.

Stop, Zora commanded in the dragon's mind.

His formidable will pushed against hers.

Turn away.

The grand dragon snorted loudly. One of his front paws clawed the dirt, and he shook his neck.

The voice of the Risker riding the dragon came from the woodland. "What is wrong with you, beast? Onward!"

Zora locked on the dragon's thoughts. He was restless

and angry, fighting two masters at once. She spotted the Risker riding on the dragon's back. The human had a dragon charm hanging from a heavy chain about his neck like an amulet. The fiery gem burned brightly as he fought against the dragon's reins. The Risker clutched the amulet, moving his head from side to side, and his gaze fell right on Zora's hiding spot.

"Well, well!" the Risker said. "It seems we've found another dragon charm wielder. Please, reveal yourself. I desire to see the face of my enemy."

The second dragon slunk alongside the first. He had a human woman rider with a similar dragon charm amulet around her neck. She spotted Zora. "We have found our prey. Interesting."

"She uses a charm against mine, Nevna," the warrior said.

"I can see that, Crufus," the dark-eyed woman said. "But our two charms are superior to her one."

An intense beam of pink light streaked over Zora's head, struck Nevna in the chest, and knocked her from the saddle.

Zora turned around.

Tatiana marched down the hill with the Star of Light smoking in her hand. Behind her, all members of Talon charged like wild-eyed madmen toward the dragons.

"Long live the Monarchy!" Beak and Tinison screamed.

"Keep that dragon locked up, Zora," Tatiana said. "We'll handle the others."

Leading the charge, Gorva flew down the hill and launched her spear.

The shaft sailed true and struck the second grand dragon in the eye. An explosion of flames burst from the dragon's mouth, scorching the earth and spreading up the hill.

Tatiana used the Star of Light, lifting her friends above the flames. They sailed across the hill, hands filled with steel, and landed on Nevna and her dragon. Tatiana stood her ground by Zora's side. "You can do it, Zora. Command that dragon!"

The dragon bucked, tossing Razor, Beak, and Tinison off of its back. He lashed out with his tail, knocking their legs out from under them, then clawed the spear out of his eye. The scales on his chest turned the color of fire, and steam came out of his nose.

"Everybody, move!" Razor yelled. He pushed Beak one way and Tinison the other then turned and dove down the hill with dragon fire licking at his boots. At the bottom, he lifted his face out of the dirt and said, "That was close."

The sound of a sword scraping reached him, and Razor turned over in time to see a sharp blade coming down to split his face. He parried hard, rolled away, and jumped to his feet. He stood face-to-face with Nevna the Risker.

"Allow me to introduce myself. I'm Reginald the Razor. Nice to meet you."

The attractive woman had a calm demeanor. Her open-faced dragon helm came down to the top of her eyes. She returned a cocky smile and said, "Ah, a man who likes to play." She pulled out a dagger that matched her sword. "I'm going to enjoy this."

He unsheathed his dagger, matching her weapons with his. "You'd better enjoy it, because it won't last long."

Nevna pounced like a leopard, clipping his shoulder and drawing first blood. Their swords locked against their chests. She got close enough to kiss him and replied, "You're right about that. It won't last long."

Zora was engaged in a wrestling match with Crufus. The Risker had a strong tie with his dragon, making it impossible to break. She tried sending soothing thoughts to the dragon's mind, gaining his confidence. But Crufus cut the effort off and pushed back.

"Kill them, Blaze Setter!" Crufus demanded. "Obey my command and kill them all!"

Zora fired back her own thoughts.

You don't have to do this, Blaze Setter. Disown your master. Be free.

Blaze Setter reared and roared. He shook his head like a dog shedding water. When his feet hit the ground, the trees shook. With a snort, he locked his gaze on Zora and Tatiana and stormed up the hill.

An arc of light streaked out of Tatiana's palm and smote the dragon between the horns. The dragon slid backward, sank his claws into the earth, and surged back up the hill.

"I can't stop them," Tatiana said. She crouched beside Zora. "They're too big and too strong." She lifted her arm, forming a radiant dome shield around her. "This won't hold forever. Only you can stop him."

Blaze Setter and Crufus loomed over them. The dragon lowered his horns and rammed the dome, which started to crack. Chips of it started to fall.

Tatiana's face drew tight. Her arms shook against the dragon's might.

The dragon drew a breath and unleashed a stream of fire.

"Zora, hurry!" Tatiana's face beaded with sweat. Her body trembled. Dragon fire engulfed the dome. The air around them started to heat, suffocating them.

28

GORVA JUMPED ACROSS THE GROUND, snatched up her spear, and rolled to her feet in one fluid motion. She struck Nevna's dragon behind the wing, piercing the softer scales.

The brute beast roared. His huge body swung around, tail whipping behind him and breaking through small trees and branches. Fluid oozed from his wounded eye. The other burned with murder. He summoned his flame.

"Come on, dragon! I don't fear your fire!" she said.

Flames spit out of the monster's mouth.

Gorva leaped like a lizard, high above the earth-scorching fire. She hurled another spear at the dragon's other eye, piercing him deep into the skull.

Roaaar!

The dragon thrashed about like a bull gone mad. His

body crashed into trees, splintering them and making loud cracking sounds.

Gorva, Beak, and Tinison moved out of the monster's path.

"Is he dying?" Beak asked. She was breathing heavily, and her sword arm trembled. "I hope so. I've hit him a dozen times, and he doesn't bleed."

"You need a sharper sword," Gorva said.

"Agreed."

Tinison knelt, panting. "I'm exhausted. And I think that thing is getting madder. At least he can't see us."

The dragon raked the spear out of his eye, turned toward them, and drew in a breath. In a cavernous voice, he said, "I don't need to see you. I can smell you. I can hear you. I will taste you. My wounds will heal, but yours will last forever."

"Great. He talks," Tinison said as he rose back to his feet. "And he's cocky." He took a breath. "Well, no better time to die than the present." He lifted his sword and screamed, "For the Monarchy!"

Metal clashed against metal. Steel glinted in the sun.

Razor jumped to the side, evading Nevna's slashing sword. He counterthrust, and his blade skipped off the side of her breastplate.

Standing face-to-face, they exchanged a flurry of strokes. *Bang. Clang. Swing. Crash.*

Nevna proved to be every bit the swordswoman she appeared, truly worthy of the title of Risker. She had a strong sword arm and natural instincts, and she attacked without fear.

Razor backed away and let his sword and dagger hang at his side.

"What's the matter, Reginald the Razor? Do you tire?" Nevna taunted.

"No," he replied, wiping the blood from his cheek where she'd nicked him. "I thought I'd give you a chance to surrender."

With a playful expression in her dark eyes, she said, "How amusing."

"I'm only trying to be fair. You see, this little sparring session, well, I was probing you for weakness. For example, you tuck your shoulder before you strike and spread your feet out a little too far. Those are only a couple of your flaws."

Nevna's jaw tightened. "I could say the same about you."

"Me? I don't think so. I don't have a weakness. My sword skill is flawless."

"Really?' She raised her eyebrows. "Perhaps I should surrender." She sheathed her dagger, dipped her finger into her belt, and threw a small globe at him.

The globe shattered, bathing Razor in blinding light.

"Augh!" His eyes burned, and he couldn't see a thing. "Are you a swordswoman or a witch?"

"Both," she said. "Prepare to meet the grave, Reginald the Razor."

"Hurry, Zora! You must control this dragon!" Tatiana pleaded. She was down on her knees with her arms raised, clutching the Star of Light in a white-knuckled grip. The dome of energy continued to collapse.

Zora was balled up on the ground, holding the charm and trying to block out the suffocating heat. She couldn't think or speak.

The flames died down. Smoke and steam rose from the energy of the dome. Crufus and his dragon faded behind the haze.

Zora looked at Tatiana's exhausted face and asked, "Are they gone?"

The dome sparked and fizzled. No sign of the Risker could be seen through the haze.

"I don't know," Tatiana said. "Did you use the charm?"

She shook her head. "I lost my concentration." Her clothing was soaked in sweat. She wiped her damp hair away from her eyes. "Let me try to connect with it again."

She cradled the charm in both of her palms and closed her eyes.

Wham!

Blaze Setter rammed the dome with his horns.

Wham! Wham! Wham!

The dome cracked and started to fade.

Tatiana's legs wobbled. She swooned and fell to the ground.

Crufus raised his dragon charm amulet in triumph. He pointed down at Zora. "Your fall now comes!"

Something whistled over Zora's head. She caught a glimpse of a long-handled axe flipping end over end. It cracked against the brim of Crufus's helmet and knocked him out of the saddle.

The mountain man West lifted Zora to her feet. "Whatever you have to do, girlie, do it now." He shielded her from the dragon. "My skin ain't fireproof!"

Blaze Setter knocked West aside with his front paw. The mountaineer hit a tree with a crack and sagged down to the forest floor.

With a trembling hand holding the dragon charm, Zora stood before the dragon. "Stay back," she said in a shaky voice. "Go away."

The charm's fire had long extinguished. It was nothing more than a pretty rock.

I can't connect with it. Please work.

Blaze Setter lowered his head and eyed her. With

breath hotter than a warm summer day, he asked, "What's the matter, little one? Can you no longer use your trinket?"

She shook her head. Her limbs locked up. She wanted to run but couldn't move.

"What a shame," he said with smoke streaming out of his nostrils. "What a shame indeed." He slowly opened up his jaws and advanced.

29

RAZOR DROPPED HIS DAGGER, drew another long sword, and swung blindly. He tried to blink the dark spots from his eyes. "No surprise that you fight like a coward."

Nevna's laugh was low and scoffing. "Ah, but where are your boasts now?"

He caught the sound of her boots scuffling over the ground toward him and unleashed a sword stroke. Metal rang against metal. "I'm blind, and you still can't hit me. It's time you learned what a true sword master is."

"Indulge me!" Nevna thrust.

Razor batted her swing away. Though blind, he could envision her in his mind. The sounds of her feet gave away where she was. Her breathing was heavy. The leather inside her armor rubbed against the metal. Razor knew what she was going to do the moment she started to move. He lunged, delivering sword stroke after sword stroke.

Her steel crashed against his. She blocked his aggressive assault, backpedaled, and tried to counter. "Impossible!"

"You've been wasting too much time riding dragons." Razor turned up his attack, forcing her to shuffle backward and parry for her life. "When you should have been practicing."

"No!" She knocked both of his blades aside with a backhanded stroke then lunged with her dagger and planted it in his ribs. Standing toe-to-toe with him, she said, "It is you who underestimates me. How does that feel?"

Razor headbutted her in the chin. "I've had worse." He spun his right blade around, brought it down fast, and severed her sword arm above the wrist.

"Augh!"

Razor put his shoulder into his second strike and buried his sword deep in her shoulder. He heard her stagger away as his vision began to clear. Then Nevna turned and ran into the cover of the trees.

He looked down at the dagger sticking in his stomach. "Huh, maybe I haven't had worse." He pulled it out, tossed it aside, found a tree to lean against, and sat down. The clamor of his friends fighting for their lives was the last thing he heard before his vision started to fade and turn black.

With a swipe of his tail, Nevna's dragon sent Tinison flying over the ground and crashing into the tree limbs.

Beak stood with her sword ready and gave Gorva a doubtful look.

Gorva mouthed, "Don't move." If the dragon couldn't see them or hear them, then they had a better chance to attack. She reached for Beak's sword.

Beak shook her head.

Gorva needed a weapon, but the honor guard made it clear she wasn't about to give hers up. She shook her head and drew her dagger. It would have to do.

The dragon crouched on all fours, sniffing and tilting his head from side to side. "You think you can hide from me? There is nowhere to hide once I have your scent, and I have them both." He licked his chops. "I'm going to enjoy crunching on your bones and grinding them up like powder. Mmm."

Gorva moved in front of Beak and said, "Let me handle this."

"Ah, the bold one that wounded me speaks. I shall devour you first," the dragon said.

The sky rumbled. A bolt of energy ripped through the trees and smote the dragon behind the wings. His bones lit up beneath his scales, and he let out a roar of pain.

Gorva spotted an opening to strike and started

forward, but a long-haired woman in glistening dragon armor dropped through the branches. Anya landed right between the dragon's horns. With lightning in her eyes, she jammed her glimmering sword deep into the dragon's skull.

Anya said in a husky voice, "Clear out," then jumped away.

Lightning struck from above, hitting the embedded sword and blowing the dragon's skull apart. Dragon scales, bones, and bits rained down on them.

Anya stood with her hands on her hips, laughing.

Blaze Setter's jaws closed in. Zora crouched under his shadow.

The roar of another dragon shook the earth, and Cinder descended from the sky. He sank his teeth into Blaze Setter's neck and clamped down.

Both dragons tumbled down the slope with talons and tails entangled. Trees shattered against their girth. Huge branches broke against their backs like twigs.

Cinder did not relent. He clung to Blaze Setter and turned loose his flame. Fire spread through Blaze Setter's neck and exploded out of his eyes and mouth. The innards of his mind were turned to ash. His body slackened, and he died at Cinder's feet.

Cinder lifted his head to the sky and let out a deafening roar.

Though she was trembling like a leaf, Zora started to regain her composure. "I can't do this," she said and dropped the dragon charm.

Crane crept up behind her, making her jump.

"Whoa, you're shaking like a leaf." He picked up the dragon charm. "Now isn't the moment to be faint of heart. You bought us time and saved us all." He put the charm in her hand. "Have faith in yourself. We all do. Didn't you see all of us run down that hill? Well, I just made it, but you saw them. They fight for you. They fight for each other. If one falls, another rises, and we will win, so long as we work together. Look."

She surveyed the battle scene. The forest was a wreckage of trees, smoke, and fire. Two grand dragons were dead. The stink of their charred flesh carried on the wind. Ashes fell gently like snow.

Somewhere in the woodland, Gorva shouted for help.

30

Zora found Gorva and Beak kneeling beside Razor. He was leaning against a tree, as pale as a ghost.

Gorva held his head up and gently smacked his face. "Don't you die on me. Don't you dare die on me!"

"Tatiana!" Zora yelled.

Aided by Crane, Tatiana ambled down the hillside with an exhausted look on her face. He helped lower her to the ground by Razor.

Sitting on her knees, Tatiana rummaged through her clothing and struggled to open her belt pouch. "Help me with this."

Zora grabbed the pouch and dumped out the contents, including many potion vials. "Which one?" she asked.

Tatiana pointed at one with a cap covered in golden-yellow wax like the inside of a beehive. "That one. Make him drink it."

Gorva snatched the vial, pulled the cap free with her mouth, pinched Razor's nose, opened his mouth, and poured the contents in. She shut his mouth and held it fast. "Drink, Reginald. Drink."

"Help me," Tatiana said as she fought her way closer to Razor.

Zora assisted her in scooting along the blade master's side. "What do you need?"

"Hold me steady." Tatiana put the Star of Light against Razor's wound and pinned it with her hand. Her eyebrows knitted, and she gasped.

The Star of Light illuminated.

Tatiana pushed back against Zora. "Brace me," she said.

Gorva moved behind Tatiana and pushed her shoulders.

Blue veins rose in Tatiana's face, and she moaned. "The wound is deep."

"Tatiana, what are you doing?" Zora asked. A stab wound had opened up in Tatiana's chest. "You're hurting yourself!" She tried to knock Tatiana's arm down. "Stop it!"

Gorva shoved Zora back and growled. "Let her be!"

Tatiana panted. "It's fine." The veins vanished from her face, and the wound in her chest closed. "It's done." Then she fainted in Gorva's arms.

Razor opened his eyes and said, "Now this is what I like

to see. Me surrounded by beautiful women." He dropped his gaze on Tatiana. "What happened to her?"

"She almost died trying to save you," Gorva said.

"Huh. Well, let's not forget I almost died trying to save all of you. Looks like I did a fine job. You're welcome."

Zora dropped her head and sighed. *We survived.* She lifted her gaze and said, "You're a real piece of workmanship, Razor. I'm glad you made it."

Razor yawned and stretched out his arms. "That little devil blinded me and stuck me good. Say, where is she?'

The roar of dragon flame drowned out all other sounds. The forest heated, and the air surrounding them lit up. An agonized pair of screams was snuffed out.

Zora got to her feet and hustled up the hill. Then she slowed, covering her face from the heat of the flames.

Cinder's fire scorched the earth. The scales on his chest were heated like hot coals, but they started to dim, and his flame went out.

A pillar of thick black smoke spiraled toward the sky. Two bodies lay in a pile of ash with hot armor melting over skeletons. The mouths of the dead were opened wide as they silently howled back at the sky.

Anya stood on the other side of the fire, holding the sky blade. Her eyes were ablaze. She took her helmet off and watched the remains of Crufus and Nevna burn.

"What have you done?" Zora asked as the others caught up with her.

"The only good enemy is a dead enemy. Today is judgment day for them," Anya replied.

"We don't kill our enemies in cold blood," Zora stated.

"Maybe you don't, but I do." Anya reached over and petted Cinder's wing. "Or we do, rather."

Tinison and West limped over and stared at the pyre.

"Whoa," Tinison said. He looked up at Cinder. "You melted that armor like wax. I like it!"

"Agreed," Razor continued. "They would have only tried to escape and kill us again."

"Brutal, I say," West added. "And glorious at the same time."

Zora shook her head. Everyone's blood was still charged from the heat of battle, but the Riskers had it coming. They all did if they didn't turn from their ways. She only wished she could have questioned them.

"What's done is done," she said. "Make sure everyone is present and accounted for. We still have a long journey ahead."

Anya walked over with two dragon charm amulets in her hand and offered them to Zora. "To the victor go the spoils."

Zora took the amulets and put them in her satchel. "Thank you, but I don't feel like much of a victor today. If you hadn't arrived..." She choked. "I couldn't control that dragon."

"Don't overthink it. You've controlled dragons before.

You'll control them again." Anya placed her helmet back on and buckled the chin strap. "Cinder and I will see to it the way is clear. If you need us, Tatiana can reach out the same as she did this time."

"Tatiana!" They had abandoned the sorceress at the bottom of the hill. When Zora looked back, West was carrying her in his arms.

"You forgot one," the mountaineer said. "Quite a sight for a woman. I can carry her until she wakes. Don't mind a bit."

"Thank you, West. And thank you for helping," Zora said.

"Never fought a dragon before. Now I live to tell about it. What a glorious day!" He peered at Tatiana. "In a variety of ways."

Cinder nudged Zora as Anya climbed into his saddle. "You did well, Zora. Don't lose your confidence. Everybody fails sometimes."

"Not me," Anya stated.

Zora petted Cinder's nose and said, "See you soon."

He nodded. "I'm looking forward to it."

31

BANCED UP BUT NOT BROKEN, Talon began the arduous trek into the Peaks of Ugrad. Led by their surefooted guide, West, they marched through wind and rain. The ravines in the hills spread out like veins, creating a labyrinth.

West led them through abandoned mining trails that cut through the rocks. They passed tunnel entrances that were covered in overgrowth. Some rock formations looked like giant men. The cries of eagles carried over the wind.

Zora's thighs and ankles burned. West moved at a brisk pace, leading the way with a hoop of rope thrown over his shoulder. She looked down the hill. They were so far up that the treetops of the Black Foothills were tiny.

It's a good thing we left Crane behind, or we'd never make it.

Crane wasn't the only one left behind either. Tinison's

ribs were broken. They'd bandaged him up and left him with Crane, despite Tinison's adamant bickering.

"I'm not going to rot like a log at the bottom of this hill," the honor guard said. "I'm going."

When he spat blood, he changed his mind. "Maybe not."

They came upon a narrow bridge of rock that crossed over a steep ravine.

West started to unspool his rope. "I'll go across first. We'll use the rope to guide you over." He handed one end to Razor and started across.

The bridge was no wider than the man's shoulders but rounded off on the sides.

Razor leaned over the ravine and said, "I can't even see the bottom. And I can't help but wonder what would possess a person to go this direction in the first place."

"What do you mean?" Gorva asked.

"Seems like a waste of time is all," Razor replied.

West yelled back from the other side of the one-hundred-foot expanse. "I'm a mountaineer! It's what I do!" He secured the rope to a tree on the other side. "Do the same!"

"Says the man with ears as big as a jackrabbit's." Razor tied the rope to a tree branch.

"That doesn't look like a good knot," Gorva said. She shoved him. "Here, let me do it."

"My knot is fine."

Shaking her head, Beak said, "That doesn't look like a good knot to me either. What sort of knot is that?"

Razor gave her a befuddled look. "It's a half hitch."

"It's not a half hitch. It's not even a knot. It's a bunch of loops."

"It's fine!" West yelled. He jerked the rope, and Razor's knot tightened to perfection.

"See? I told you it was good."

Gorva and Beak inspected the rope and shook their heads in disbelief.

"Come over one at a time. No telling how much the bridge will hold. I've only crossed it alone myself," West said.

Tatiana went first, crossing quickly. Beak and Gorva went next, moving over the bridge with little trouble.

Razor said to Zora, "After you."

"I think you should go first."

"Sorry, but I don't leave women and children behind."

"You're scared, aren't you?"

"No." He peered down at the ravine. "But I don't like deep ravines, ropes, or bridges."

"You'll make it. Go quickly." Zora hooked her arm around the rope and made her way across the rock bridge. The rope was as taut as a bowstring and held like a cord of iron.

What is this made of?

She didn't slip once as she traversed the rounded edges

of the bridge. She even put her weight on the rope a few times. "It's solid, Razor. Hang on to the rope. It will hold."

Razor tugged on the rope and eased out onto the bridge. On the other side, everyone stared at him.

"Quit gawking!"

"What are you scared of?" Gorva asked. "It's a simple trek."

He eased out a few dozen feet. "Well, falling is the first thing that comes to mind." His breathing was rapid and shallow. He looked down and swooned. "And I get a queasy feeling when there's no ground under me."

"You've ridden a dragon," Zora said. "And there's no ground beneath it."

"That's different." He shuffled over the bridge to the halfway point, puffing. "I don't like this, and I didn't care for that much either."

"You're almost here. Don't look down," Gorva suggested.

Razor leaned on the rope, closed his eyes, and caught his breath. His heart pounded. He didn't fear anything but heights. He'd climbed a tree as a little boy with his older brothers, and they'd coaxed him into jumping from one branch to another. He was scared and too short to make the jump, but he tried anyway. He didn't make it halfway across. His brothers reached for him, but their outstretched arms weren't long enough. He landed back first on a branch then hit the ground flat on his back. He was numb for weeks yet finally healed, but he never forgot his parents talking about having to take him away to a place for the crippled and broken. He'd grown up hearing his brothers telling horror stories about it.

He opened his eyes. His rushing blood drowned out his comrades' voices. He could just make out the bottom of the ravine. Something big and wild slunk in the darkness.

"I'm coming." Shuffling over one step at a time, he made it across two-thirds of the bridge.

His friends urged him on, and he looked back and smiled.

Then the mountain quaked, and the bridge gave out beneath him. Rocks crashed into the ravine.

Razor hung on to the rope with both hands, his feet dangling over the ravine. He closed his eyes and froze.

32

"Razor, get moving. You can't hang on forever!" Gorva said.

"I'm trying!" he yelled back then cracked an eye open. "Ooh. I like the view better with my eyes closed."

"Go forward, Reginald, before you lose your strength. Your gear is too heavy," Gorva warned him.

"I know that." He started moving toward the other side, stretching out hand over hand. His fingers started to burn, and with every foot he crossed, his body became heavier. He picked up speed and mumbled, "I'm going to make it. I'm going to make it."

"Come on! Come on!" Talon urged him.

Thirty feet became twenty-five, twenty-five became twenty, and twenty became fifteen.

"Almost there." He panted and licked the salt from his lips. His shoulders burned, and he fought to keep his grip.

"I'm getting this over with." He locked his jaw and moved forward.

Thwip! A slimy tongue shot up from the bowels of the ravine and coiled around Razor's ankle.

"Guh! What is that?"

A toad the size of a horse clung to the ravine wall a couple dozen feet below. Its slimy tongue started to tow him down.

"Somebody kill that thing!"

"Mountain toad," West said. "Very big. Very dangerous." He stood on the edge and peered down the ravine wall. "I'll be back." Then he jumped.

Razor's shoulders and hips jolted. It felt like the bones were being pulled from their sockets. "Augh!"

West stood on the toad's head, butchering it in the face with his axes. He got a clean shot on its tongue and sliced right through it. The toad widened its jaws and sucked West halfway into its mouth. It detached from the wall, and they descended into darkness.

New energy fed strength into Razor's limbs. Hand over hand, he moved to the other side of the bridge. Gorva grabbed him the first chance she had and hauled him in.

Razor dropped to his knees and kissed the ground. "Thank goodness that's over." He caught everyone looking over the ledge. "We lost our guide, didn't we?"

"I believe so," Zora replied.

"No, you didn't," West shouted up from the ravine.

"He's climbing up the wall!" Beak said in amazement.

Razor started toward the ledge, stopped, and said, "I'll take your word for it."

With the help of the others, West swung his body over the brim. They patted him on the back.

"That was astonishing," Zora said. "But that thing was eating you. How did you survive?"

"It wouldn't be the first time a hungry toad took a crack at me. Lucky for me, when we hit the ground, its body had some cushion in it. Plus, when you're a mountain man"— he winked at Beak—"you get used to falling from time to time. Some falls are harder than others."

"Glad you made it," Razor said.

West grabbed his rope and said, "Glad you made it too." He tugged once on the rope, and it came loose on the other side of the ravine. He spooled it up in seconds. "If all is well, let's resume our journey before nightfall. That's when the most dangerous creatures attack."

Talon camped on the inside of a large cave that was tucked away in the ominous peaks. The weary party cooked strips of salted beef over a fire and drank from wineskins.

Razor lay on his side, chewing his dinner, while the others huddled around the fire. "How much farther?" he asked.

"We'll be there in a couple of days." West tore his meat apart with his fingers and started to eat. "Good beef."

"I don't guess there are any shortcuts?" Razor asked.

"This is the shortest route. Any other way would be days longer and little safer. We could change direction, if you wish. I enjoy the climb," he said.

"No, no, no. The sooner, the better." Razor drank from his skin. "The sooner we get up the mountain, the sooner we can start back down."

"Assuming you return," West replied. He caught everyone looking at him. "I'm not trying to spook you, but the Flaming Fence is buried under these hills for a reason. I've seen the Cavity. Wandered into its midst. Saw the door of fire. I have no desire to venture any closer than I have." He rubbed his hairy arms. "I get the goose bumps thinking about it."

Zora sat with her knees pulled to her chest, looking into the fire. "How did you find it in the first place?"

"I've lived near the peaks all my life. Raised in the mines and timber camps. Ever since I could remember, I wanted to climb the great rock." West licked his fingers and wiped them on his shirt. "As I grew older, I heard about the Flaming Fence. A legend. But my forefathers swore its doorway nested in these desecrated hills. They'd seen it. Or so the story went. There are many tall tales about the Peaks. I've heard them all."

He scooted closer to the fire and grabbed another stick of meat.

"I decided I wanted to find it for myself. After all, I love these hills, the climb, and its creatures. I'd spent years rambling across the ledges. Why not spend years trying to find everything it has to offer? No one knows the Peaks better than me. Ask anyone."

"You mean to tell me you spent years searching for something that might not even be there?" Razor asked. He chucked his stick into the fire. "All alone in these hills. No, thanks."

"There's nothing odd about that," Beak said. She'd moved closer to West while he was talking. "Treasure hunters do it all the time."

"But he wasn't finding treasure. He was finding death's door."

"I think it's passionate," Beak said.

Razor rolled over, putting his back to the fire. He yawned and said, "Keep that passion burning. I have a feeling we're going to need it."

"Aye, get your rest," West replied. "You'll need all of your energy for the journey into the Chasm of Chaos."

CHAPTER 33—THE PAST

STREAK GLIDED ABOVE THE CLOUDS, wings spread wide, with the cold air nipping his snout and the bright sun kissing his face. He dove through pillowy fields of cotton and popped out on the other side then skimmed beneath the white haze. The gray clouds covered the land, making for another dreary day.

Snow fell on the fields and valleys east of Valley Shire. The snow on the ground was light, but the mountain caps were covered. Winter had come. Though mild in the south, it still made for a frosty landscape early in the morning before the full sun took it away.

Many seasons had passed since Zanna Paydark betrayed Grey Cloak and Dyphestive, turning the blood brothers to stone and abandoning them. Streak was left behind to protect them. He'd been alone ever since.

He flicked his pink tongue out of his mouth, tasting snowflakes one at a time. "Fruity. Sour. Bland. Bland. Bland. Doughy. Ah, who am I fooling? They all taste the same."

He dipped a little deeper toward the land, keeping his eyes open for the enemy, while dragging his twin tails behind him.

He had seen no sign of Zanna. She'd taken Grey Cloak's gear, including the Rod of Weapons and the Cloak of Legends, and all but vanished. She'd said she needed to retrieve a scroll to free the brothers from the Wizard Watch, but that hadn't happened.

What if something happened to her? What if I need to rescue her? If she's gone, who's going to save them? Speaking of which, I'd better head back.

Streak's travels took him across the great river, toward Littleton and back. He'd even flown farther back east, toward the Wizard Watch, more times than he could count. At the watchtower, from a distance, he waited. No one, not one single person, ever went in or came out.

He flew for hours toward the high hills where the blood brothers were permanently stationed. When he spotted the hills, he dove toward the snow-covered pines and landed on the ridge that overlooked the western fields.

The camp the brothers had set up was covered in overgrowth. The firepits, long cold, were nothing more than snow-covered dirt. The cabin still stood with its back against the hills. Its log walls held, but it was covered in vegetation. Critters and birds nested inside the shelter, making a mess. All of the rations had long since been devoured.

Streak sat down in front of Grey Cloak and Dyphestive. He could see little underneath the grimy buildup, but the brothers' frozen faces were full of surprise, and their mouths were open in anguish. Moss grew on them, covering the side with the most shade. Vines of ivy covered most of the bodies. The seeds of trees they'd cleared years ago had sprung up all around them.

A pair of red-breasted robins landed on Grey Cloak's head and shoulder and immediately took a quick poop.

"Will you go away?" Streak fluttered his wings, scattering the birds. "How would you like it if someone did that to you? Little pests." He eyed his master. "Sorry about that, boss. I've tried to keep you cleaned up, but I think blending in with the elements is better. That way, you aren't very likely to be seen."

He sighed.

"I've been looking for Zanna, as I always do, but she's nowhere to be found. But she'll be back. I'm sure." He sat down like a dog. "I don't know if you can tell, but I've grown more. Getting bigger and hungrier. I've tried to hibernate, but a big bear stole my cave. I thought I'd let him be, in case I want to eat him later."

He turned toward Dyphestive. He was literally a

boulder of muscle.

"I hope you aren't suffering. I hope it's only like sleep. I think Zanna said it was like that, but she didn't give me a lot of comfort." Using his tail, he brushed some grit from Grey Cloak's face. "Boy, I bet you're mad. I bet you want to kill her. But she thinks you didn't give her a choice. At least not after the run-in with the Bedlam Brothers. Good news, though. No one has shown up to come and look for us after the first time. All is quiet. And lonely."

Streak always told the same stories, day and night, and shared with them everything he'd seen. Deep inside, he felt his voice would comfort them, and he did the best he could.

The cry of birds came over the hills, and he looked toward the sky. Scavenger birds circled, not too far away. "I wonder what that's all about. I'll be back. Don't go anywhere. Uh, no pun intended."

Streak stole into the hills with the stealth of a mountain lion. Over the years, he'd honed his hunting skills and learned to navigate the woodland like any other creature in its natural habitat. His claws found purchase on the rocks, and he climbed higher until he found a spot overlooking the area where the birds of prey were circling.

Over a hundred feet below, on a bare patch, a man was sprawled out on the ground, not moving. His body was pierced by many arrows.

Streak sniffed and said, "I smell trouble."

34

THE PUNGENT SMELL of eroding flesh permeated the air. Whoever had died on the hill had been there long enough to draw the attention of hungry varmints and scavengers but not long enough for them to dive in. Something lurked in the woods. It spooked them.

Regardless, Streak didn't like the smell of it. Someone had invaded the tranquil hills, and they reeked of trouble. He moved down the hill at a slow pace, not stirring so much as a branch, then reached a flat peak and hid among the thickets.

The dead man looked like a scarecrow for target practice. He wore heavy clothing with armor underneath, and his bare feet had been stripped clean. Snow covered most of his body and the bloody trail where he had fallen. He lay chest down on the ground, head twisted and one eye open. In his frozen grip was a strip of parchment.

"Looks like someone had a bad day," Streak said.

The snow held many boot impressions. There were big paw prints too. It appeared that a small party had over-taken the man and put him down like a hunted animal.

Streak tasted the air. The men who'd invaded the wood-land moved fast. Their tracks started on a path up the hill and vanished in the cover of the trees.

He shrugged his wings and said, "Ah, I've got nothing better to do," then went after them. "And I can't have them wandering into my camp, anyway. The hill is mine."

The invaders' tracks weren't difficult to follow. Streak's, on the other hand, were a different matter. His tracks would stick out like a sore thumb, so he used his twin tails to brush over everything he passed.

By the time he caught up with the party of invaders, night had fallen, and they'd made camp on a wide stretch of ground at the base of the next peak.

Streak flanked them, moving across the stones to a higher position within earshot of their camp. Then he hunkered down and became one with the stones.

One of the wolves howled. Two of the beasts looked toward Streak and started barking. The wolves were huge, and their fur was black. Their backs stood as high as the waist of the man yanking on their leashes.

"Heel!" the man said. He was strong in stature and

covered in a heavy wool coat, and a quiver of arrows was slung over his shoulder. He peered in Streak's direction but saw right through him. "If there's something out there, it ain't bothering us." He spat. "We'll eat it if it does."

"Trouble," another man said. He lingered with his hands over the flames.

"Naw. The wolves are spooked, is all. Are you making any sense of that map yet?"

"Eh, I got it."

"You'd better, after we had to kill our guide."

The man by the fire rubbed his hands over the flames and said, "He got us to where we didn't need him anymore. Besides, he got greedy."

"Aye."

Streak counted four men by the fire, excluding the one handling the wolves. Two tents were set up in their camp, and rough sacks and gear lay on the ground.

"You really overdid it with Morley," one of the other men said. He appeared to be sipping coffee from a steel cup. "Why waste all of those arrows on him? Did he give you a cross look?"

"Almost," the wolf handler said.

The roughnecks chuckled. Their hot breath steamed in the cold air.

Streak's scales rose. *These aren't good men.*

One of them cleared his throat loudly and spat. "What do you think, Egon? We going to find this lair tomorrow?"

The man with the map leaned over the campfire. His frosty hair hung over one of his eyes. "We're almost on top of it now, Chubb, by the looks of things. Somewhere on the top of that peak, we'll find an entrance."

"Assuming we find it," the wolf handler said.

"You're the one who killed Morley, Bruton. So don't start your bickering about something we ain't even started to find yet," the last man, who was as round as a barrel, said.

"Watch your tone, or you'll be next, Chinns."

Streak noticed the layers of fat underneath the beefy man's jaw. *Chinns. That's funny.*

"I liked Morley!" Chinns fired back. "We were friends going way back."

"He was a greedy moron. Gonna stab us in the back the first chance he had," Bruton said. "Nah, I didn't trust him, and even a fool like you shouldn't trust him either."

"That's enough," Egon, clearly the leader, said. "What's done is done. It happens. We don't need to start bickering over treasure we've yet to see." He rolled up his map and grunted. "As for Morley, well, I agree. He was a bad egg. Something stank about him, and he got all jittery."

The men fell silent for a bit, then Chubb asked, "What about the dragon?"

Streak perked up. *Dragon? What dragon?*

"Don't start with the dragon talk," Bruton replied. "Morley got in your head."

"No, he wasn't the only one that talked about a dragon. The folks in the village seen one too. Says he lives in these climbs," Chinns replied. "Guards the treasure, he does."

Bruton spat. "You believe everything you hear, don't you?"

"No. But I've seen dragons."

"And Riskers," Chubb added.

"We've all seen 'em. Don't mean they're hiding out in the middle of nowhere. The Riskers control the dragons, and they have it all. Living in the pleasure of the cities. That's what I'd be doing."

"You, a Risker?" Chubb laughed. "All you are is lord of the mangy hounds."

"Watch your tongue!" Bruton fired back.

"That's enough!" Egon lifted a crossbow plated with metal that caught the firelight. "Dragon or no dragon, whatever guardian might watch the treasure lair, I'll be ready for it."

35

LED BY EGON, the small band of brigands resumed their climb shortly after the break of dawn. Gusts blew the snow from the treetops, covering the men.

"Oy, I hate snow," Bruton said. The wolves strained against their restraints, pulling their master up the hill, and he gave the leashes a hard yank. "Heel! I'm a man, not a sleigh!"

The black wolves slowed, but they sniffed, whimpered, and stuffed their noses in the ground.

Egon knocked the fresh snow off of his clothes. "What's the matter with your dogs?"

"I don't know. They want to hunt something. Probably sniffed out a varmint or mountain goat." Bruton pulled back on his leashes again. "Take a rest, you mangy mutts!

It's too early for this bull." He glared back at Chinns. "And I didn't have my coffee, thanks to someone spilling it."

The large, doughy-faced man fired back, "You bumped into me, not I into you. I offered you mine."

"I'm not drinking after a bumbling fool."

Streak followed the company and kept them in his line of sight and within earhole shot. He tried to stay downwind, but the breeze shifted from time to time.

These guys are hilarious.

He'd been watching them all morning. The men bickered, cursing the snow and folding their tents, which they'd doubled up in. From his hiding spot, Streak got a closer look at the company.

They were a gritty bunch, messy-haired and hard-eyed. The big ones, Chinns and Chubb, wore oversize coats made of buffalo skin. They appeared to be more muscle than brain, and they carried short bows, quivers of arrows, and clubs. The large packs on their shoulders made them look more like pack mules than men, and based on their flat noses and jutting chins, they probably had orcen blood in them. Chinns was more slack-jawed and heavy.

Egon and Bruton were a different sort, better put together. Both wore long woolen overcoats. They were full-blooded men, bossy and quick to take command. Egon had long, frosty locks, and his tan skin was weathered and full of wrinkles. His harsh voice bit like the chilly wind.

"There!" Egon pointed at one of the peaks. "That's our marker."

Chinns squinted and said, "I don't see anything,"

"Look at that crag. It's shaped like a perched hawk. That's the spot," Egon stated.

"I don't see it," Chinns repeated.

"Neither do I," Chubb added.

Bruton huffed. "It doesn't matter if you're too stupid to see it or not. Clam up and follow!"

Streak didn't have any trouble spotting the rock formation jutting out of the peaks. It stuck out like a sore thumb.

Huh. It does look like a hawk overlooking the valley.

The rock had the body of a large bird with its wings closed, a head at the top, and a beak. The peaks leaned over it, shielding the formation from the wind and snow.

"Ah, I see it now. Kind of pretty," Chinns said. "Where do we go from here?"

Egon swung his crossbow from one shoulder to the other and said, "The entrance should be on the top of that peak."

"That's quite a climb. How do you know that's the right one? There's hundreds of peaks," Chubb said.

Bruton looked like he was going to burst out of his skin. "Fool!" He pointed at the crag. "That's our marker."

Chubb touched his lips and looked at the hawk-shaped rock formation. "Oh. That makes sense." A snowball blasted him in the face. He wiped it off and glared at Bruton. "What did you do that for?"

"Because you're an idiot! And the next time you say something stupid, it won't be a snowball. It will be an arrow."

Chubb gulped.

Streak grinned. *I like these guys. Bad but in a funny way.*

In silence, the company made the agonizingly steep climb to the top, using a rope to help tow them.

Streak lost sight of them in the channels they took up the hill. He opted to scale the stony peaks using his claws then caught up with the company at the top and hid behind the stones.

"This is it," Egon said with awe as they filed onto a small plateau surrounded by a ring of stone pylons standing upright. He took out his map and unrolled it. "Look, Bruton. The Giant's Crown. We're standing on it."

Streak tilted his head. The natural rocks made a ring shaped like a crown. The stones varied in size, some taller or shorter than others, but all were between ten and twenty feet tall.

Impressive. The morons might have found something.

"What do we do now?" Chinns asked. He caught Bruton glaring at him and clammed up.

Egon squinted at his map. The wind rustled the page, so he moved to one of the stones and placed the map against it. He read aloud, "From the smallest horn, take fifteen paces toward the shadows, where the sun never peeks." He looked up at his comrades. "Dig there."

The shortest horn of the crown wasn't hard to find. It was a round, stubby one.

Egon moved to the mark. His eyes swept over the area, and he pointed to a shaded spot on one of the adjacent rocks, where there was a large niche big enough to crawl under. It was the only stone of its kind. "That must be it." He marched off fifteen paces. "Grab the shovels. Start digging."

36

S<small>TREAK</small> <small>YAWNED</small>. After hours of digging, nothing but cursing was going on. The brigands had dug a hole big enough for all four of them to stand in. Steam rose from their backs. The black wolves sat on the edge, peering down at the men with their heads tilting and ears twitching.

Chinns shoveled a big mound of dirt onto Bruton. His eyes grew big, and he said, "I'm sorry."

Bruton raised his shovel and advanced with a hot stare.

Egon stepped between them. "That's enough." He leaned on his shovel. "Everyone, take a rest. But keep moving, or you'll freeze up."

"Did the map happen to mention how deep the spot was?" Bruton asked.

"I can't imagine it would be much deeper." Egon tapped the ground with his shovel. "But it's down here. I know it."

Bruton wore a doubtful expression but said, "I hope you're right. All of this for nothing would stink to the heavens." He nudged Egon and pointed at Chinns and Chubb, who were helping each other out of the hole and paying them no mind. "But the hole will make a perfect grave for them."

Egon raised his bushy eyebrows. "Indeed."

Streak lifted his snow-covered head from his hiding spot.

Wait a moment. They're going to kill Chinns and Chubb. But I like those guys. Perhaps I should warn them.

Chinns and Chubb crawled out of the hole, rolled over the snow, then fought their way back to their feet, brushed the snow off of each other, and stretched their backs.

The brigands had provided Streak the most amusement he'd had in years. Most of his time he spent sleeping, sometimes for weeks or months, but when he woke, he searched for Zanna and explored. Nothing to date had been as interesting as the brigands, Chinns and Chubb in particular. The misguided pair cracked Streak up.

I wonder if they're brothers. They look like brothers.

Chinns handed out some packs of salted fish, and they all drank from the same waterskins. With the sun shining on the snow, icicles in the peaks started to drip.

Bruton tossed scraps to his wolves, took one last swig from the waterskin, and said, "Let's get on with it."

Chinns climbed down into the hole, slipped on the last step, and fell into Bruton.

Bruton shoved him. "Get off of me!" He eyed Chubb. "What are you waiting for? A ladder? Get in here."

"Make room," Chubb said.

"There's plenty of room. Jump," Bruton ordered.

Chubb took a leap into the gap. The ground gave way beneath his girth and collapsed underneath the men's feet. They screamed as the dirt floor caved in and the hole swallowed them.

The wolves were on their feet, howling at the pit with their hackles raised.

Streak rose from his position and stared at the hole. *Huh, I didn't see that coming.*

"We found it!" Egon yelled.

"Get off of me, Chubb!" Bruton commanded.

"I'm not on you. That's Chinns," Chubb said.

"Both of you big bellies need to get out of this dragon-forsaken hole and fetch the torches," Bruton said. "Woo-hoo! We found the treasure pit!"

The part-orcen men started clawing their way out of the pit. Their feet slid over the loose sides before finding purchase, and they managed to climb out then fetched two torches from their gear and lit them.

Chubb carried them over to the hole and peered down.

"Toss them down," Bruton yelled.

Chubb dropped both of them into the pit.

Bruton immediately screamed, "One at a time, stupid! Anvils! What is running inside that skull of yours?"

"Never mind it, Bruton. Come on," Egon said. "I see a tunnel."

"Listen, both of you. Get some rope ready. Stay put, and we'll be back," Bruton said and disappeared.

Chinns and Chubb stood outside with the wolves, pulling their coats tighter and staring down into the hole.

Bruton emerged no more than an hour later and half climbed out of the pit. He had a big smile on his disagreeable face. "We found a chest. It's a good-sized one." He grabbed the rope. "When I say tow, you start pulling. It's heavy." He scrambled back into the hole like a frightened gopher. A few moments later, he yelled, "Tow!"

Chinns and Chubb started pulling the rope back hand over hand. The cord had no slack in it.

"It's heavy," Chubb said with a grunt. "It must be a fortune."

They dragged a strongbox that was no more than two feet long and one foot wide. Egon and Bruton popped out behind it. They both had gold-hungry gleams in their eyes.

"Haul it out!" an elated Egon said.

Both he and Bruton started pushing the chest while the brothers pulled.

"If I didn't see it with my own eyes, I wouldn't believe it. We've found Bullseye Hendrick's hoard."

They pulled the strongbox out of the hole, and Egon and Bruton climbed out. All of the men's chests heaved as they gasped.

With his hands on his knees, Chubb said, "It's so heavy. There must be a thousand chips in there."

"More than that, I'd say," Bruton replied.

"So, was there a guardian? Did you kill it?" Chinns asked.

Egon gave a raspy laugh and said, "The only guardian was Bullseye Hendricks's grandson, and we took care of him. If the little weasel weren't so spoiled and lazy, he could have had it all to himself. No, this treasure is ours now. All ours."

Bruton grabbed a hammer that they used to drive in their tent stakes. "Shall I bust it open?"

Egon took a knee beside the chest and said, "No, wait. Let me see if it's booby-trapped first."

37

"Throw me my coat, Chinns," Egon said.

Chinns grabbed his wool coat from the ground and handed it to the brigand leader.

"Now back off." Egon took out a leather pouch from his coat and rolled it open. An assortment of metal thieves tools lay inside. "I've heard stories about Bullseye. He had treasure hidden in all sorts of places. A true bandit. But he put a death trap on every one."

Chinns and Chubb backed farther away from the chest.

Egon put a small spyglass in his eye socket then peered at the box's keyhole and picked at it with the lock with small metal tools.

"A shame we didn't find a key," Bruton said.

"Aye, a shame indeed." Egon delicately placed the two lockpicks in the keyhole. "There. I got it."

The men came closer.

"No, stay back. Picking the lock is only part of the trap. There's something else lingering in there." Egon moved to the side of the chest and placed his hand on the lid. He turned to Chinns and Chubb. "Don't stand in front of it, idjits. On second thought, maybe you should."

The brothers split apart.

Egon held his breath, opened the lid, and shrank back.

A cloud of gray mist sprayed into the air. *Phssst!*

Egon covered his mouth in his shirt and dove away.

The mist hung over the chest for several moments, then the wind picked up and took it away.

"Shoo, that was close. Did you smell that?" Egon asked. He coughed. "One big whiff of that would rot you from the inside out." He fanned his face and wiped his watery eyes. "Nasty."

The strongbox lay open before them.

Egon crawled toward it but stayed the others with his hand. "Hold on. There could always be another trap." He reached into the chest then screamed and started shaking. "Aaah!"

The men jumped away.

Egon chortled, and his stupefied men grumbled and shuffled closer.

He lifted his hand out of the strongbox and let a fistful of golden coins drop from his fingers. "Bullseye Hendricks's gold is ours, men. Come have a look!"

Bruton, Chinns, and Chubb dove toward the box and stuffed their hands into a sea of gold and silver.

A flabbergasted Chinns lifted two handfuls. "I've never seen so much wealth before. I haven't even imagined it."

Bruton rubbed his face in his handful of riches. "There's enough here to bathe in."

Egon sat down with a small pouch of coins he'd taken. He opened it and poured the contents out. Gold chips fell between his fingers. "I can't believe it. There are sacks full of them."

Streak huffed. *I'll be. It looks like these rotten eggs actually found real treasure. I guess anything can happen when you combine stupidity with determination.*

A golden gleam of sunlight reflected off the strongbox's riches.

The men pulled forth necklaces, bracelets, earrings, and other sorts of jewelry. A pair of pearl-handled daggers and a few other unique items followed.

"Should we count it?" Chubb asked.

"How are we going to divide it all up?" Chinns added.

Egon got up, tossed his treasure into the box, slapped both men on the back, and said, "Don't worry about that. There's more than enough to make all of us rich. I'll tell you what. Why don't the pair of you start counting out those sacks?" He caught Bruton's eye and gave him a subtle nod. "I'll grab our packs. It'll be easier to haul once we divide the spoils up."

Chubb and Chinns nodded. They hunkered down over the chest, engrossed in their work and giggling goofily.

Bruton picked up his bow and slid an arrow out of his quiver while Egon grabbed his crossbow and started to pull back the string. He locked the string into place, and it made a faint click that could barely be heard above the wind.

The part-orcen men were oblivious to the wicked pair of men preparing to shoot them in their backs.

Streak watched with intense anticipation. The scales on his stripes rose as the evil men's plan came together. They'd killed Morley, giving them a two-on-two ratio. If Morley had been with them, the assassination would be more difficult to pull off, so they'd taken him out early.

Man, this is just like on TV. Boy, I miss that world. I love that show with the monk in it. What was that called?

Egon dropped a bolt into the slide of his crossbow. Bruton nocked his arrow and pulled the string along his cheek. Chinns and Chubb didn't stand a chance.

Streak watched on pins and needles, fully captivated by the soon-to-be-murderous scene.

Come on, guys. Turn around. His tails swished. *Murdering mayhem! This is real! They're going to kill my friends.*

One assassin nodded to the other, and they took aim.

Streak stood from his hidden position and let out a roar.

Chinns and Chubb dove into the hole. The wolves

moved before their master, lowered their heads, and growled.

Streak climbed on top of one of the boulders that made up the Giant's Crown, in plain view.

Egon and Bruton turned their weapons on him.

"I thought you said there wasn't a guardian," Bruton said, his arms shaking. "What do we do now?"

Egon never batted an eyelash. He kept his aim on Streak and said, "Kill it."

38

"I'm going to make this really easy for you," Streak said. "You can leave this mountain alive, or you can die on it." He started toward the ground. "Your decision should be easy."

"It talks!" Bruton exclaimed. His wolves stood by his side, growling with their hackles raised. "What do we do?"

Egon came a couple of steps forward, keeping his crossbow aimed at Streak. "He's only a middling. One shot will take him out."

"Are you sure?" Bruton asked.

"Aye. I've done it before." Egon spit. "Listen, dragon, go on your way. Our business is none of yours."

"*Au contraire,*" Streak answered. "I am Bullseye Hendricks's guardian. Leave the treasure or leave in pieces."

Chinns and Chubb peeked out of the hole like a pair of gophers.

"The only one that will leave this hill in pieces, dragon, is you. We ain't leaving without this treasure," Egon warned him. His finger held fast on the trigger of his crossbow.

The weapon was an extraordinary item, unlike any Streak had ever seen. It was plated in silver metal and engraved with runes. The bolt also had runes on the tip. The only crossbow Streak had seen that was close to it was Drysis's. That device was a nasty piece of work.

"Ever wonder what might happen if you miss, Egon?" Streak asked. "Even if you hit me, chances are I won't die instantly, giving me more than enough time to kill you." Streak showed his teeth. "And let me assure you, I won't go quietly."

Egon's face tightened. "One way or the other, it's going to be me or you, dragon."

Streak lowered himself to the ground. "You might get me, but what are you going to do about Chubb and Chinns? After all, you were about to shoot them in the back before I had my say."

"What?" Chubb asked. "You foul betrayer! I knew you couldn't be trusted!"

He and his brother started to climb out of the hole.

"We should have known you'd take the treasure for yourselves."

They started to advance on Egon and Bruton.

"Listen to me, boys. This dragon's lying to you." Egon kept his aim on Streak. "Trying to split us up."

"We don't believe you." Chinns balled up his fists and started to move their way. "We aren't stupid, you know."

Bruton twisted his hips and fired an arrow into Chinns's leg.

Chinns screamed and clutched his leg. "I knew you were lying!"

Bruton reloaded his bow in the wink of an eyelash. "Get those hands up, Chubb! Or I'll send feather through you too."

Chubb slowly lifted his hands. "You're scum. The both of you."

Bruton laughed. "We're brigands. All of us are scum. Say, where'd the dragon go?"

During the commotion, Streak had snuck behind the boulders that made up the crown.

"See what you fools did?" Egon asked. "Bruton, send the wolves after him."

Bruton whistled and said, "Hunt!"

The wolves sprinted after Streak. They rounded the pillars of stone and came face-to-face with Streak. Jaws slavering, they pounced.

Streak had been waiting. His chest scales were heated, and he turned loosed a torrent of dragon flame.

The wolves' black fur burned, and they scurried away

toward their master, whining and yelping. Their flaming bodies collapsed in the snow. They howled no more.

Bruton screamed, "Nooo!" He fired his arrows one after the other into the rock shielding Streak. "I'll kill you, dragon! Show yourself!"

Streak stayed low to the ground and started blowing smoke. The haze carried into the crown like a heavy fog. The more smoke he let out, the thicker it became.

The men started coughing.

A second lens came down over Streak's eyes, and he prowled into the bowl of smoke. The scuffles and distraught shouts of the men led him right to them.

Chinns and Chubb babbled vainly, Bruton cursed and screamed, but Egon was as silent as a ghost.

The smart one's looking for me. Streak's tongue flicked out of his mouth. He tasted smoke and the men's scents. *Ah, there you are.*

Egon distanced himself from the others and stood with his back braced against one of the rocks. His crossbow was loaded on his shoulder, and he swept it back and forth.

Hmmm. He's no fool. I'll give him that much. I need a distraction.

"Where are you, dragon? I'll kill you! I'll avenge my wolves! I'll send you to the Black Pits of Gogmoor!" Bruton shouted.

Perfect.

With Bruton clearly losing his senses, it made it easy

for Streak to slide toward him. He snaked his twin tails out and yanked Bruton down by the ankles.

The man face-planted in the snow. "*Umph!*"

Streak spun around, and using his tails like a sling, he flipped Bruton across the ground. The man's body sailed into Egon's. Their skulls smacked together.

Streak scurried toward the woozy men, pinned both of them down with his front paws, and as the smoke cleared, he said, "You should have walked away."

Egon reached for his crossbow, but the bolt had been dislodged from the slide.

"That's not going to do you a whole lot of good," Streak said.

"Kiss my boots, dragon!" Egon said with a snarl. "I don't fear you!"

"A shame. A smart brigand would. Goodbye, you murderous and wicked people." Streak unleashed his flame on both of them.

The men's screams were soon suffocated by raging flames. Their foul voices could be heard no more as the dragon fire devoured them clean to the bone.

"That's that." The smoke started to rise, and the Giant's Crown cleared. "A shame we couldn't have had a more amiable outcome."

Chinns and Chubb huddled over the strongbox, stuffing their pockets with treasure.

"Ahem," Streak said.

The wide-eyed brothers turned.

"Please don't kill us, mighty dragon. We'll do anything you wish," Chubb said.

Streak shrugged his wings and replied, "I'll have to think about it."

39

CHINNS AND CHUBB gathered the remains of Egon, Bruton, and the wolves and tossed them into the hole. They even journeyed back and gathered Morley's cold, dead body and tossed it in with the bones of the others.

Shovelful by shovelful, the two brutes started filling the treasure hole back in.

Streak stood over the strongbox, watching them shovel the last loads of dirt on top of the pit.

The men's shoulders were bunched up with muscle, and they sweated profusely. But they didn't say a word or cast so much as a glance Streak's way. He had them right where he wanted them.

What am I going to do with these two dummies?

Streak didn't have it in his heart to kill them. They were misguided but not entirely wicked like Egon and Bruton.

He didn't care about the treasure either, but if they took it, they would spend it all or have their throats cut in a week. If he sent them away, they would only tell others and come back. Greed worked on stupid people that way.

I need to think of something.

Chinns packed the dirt down with the back of his shovel while Chubb leaned on his. Sweat dripped from both men's brows and soaked into the ground.

"Uh, may I eat or drink?" Chinns asked but kept his eyes averted. "I feel light-headed."

"Enjoy your rations, both of you," Streak said.

Night had fallen, and more snow came with it. Within hours, the Giant's Crown would be covered in snow, and within weeks, it would be like no one had been there in years.

Under the moonlight, the brothers huddled close together and ate quietly. They put on their coats as the temperature dropped. Each of them stole a quick glance over his shoulder at Streak or the treasure chest from time to time.

They're still thinking about how to get it. Greed. It wouldn't be a good story without it.

Streak decided to strike up a conversation. "So, if you had all of this treasure, what would you do with it?"

"I would get a woman. A beautiful one," Chubb said.

Chinns hit his brother in the arm. "No, he wouldn't. We'd buy farmland and take wives. Good ones."

"Really? Are you sure you wouldn't celebrate? Gamble and drink in the company of harlots?"

They vigorously shook their heads.

"No, no, we'd never do something like that," Chinns said. "We're honest men doing honest work."

"If that's the case, how did you come to work with Egon and Bruton?"

"They needed strong backs, and we needed money. We always need money. Been poor all of our lives," Chinns said with his eyes downcast.

"Uh-huh. But I was of the impression you were part of a band of brigands. Sounds to me like you've been brigands for some time. Brigands rob and hassle innocent people."

Chubb nodded. "Aye. We've done all of those things."

"Hush, Chubb," Chinns said.

"No, it's the truth. We've been robbing all our lives. Since we was children," Chubb continued. "We don't know another way. This is how we live." He eyed the chest. "But with the gold, our lives will change. We won't have to rob anyone again."

"Aside from the man you stole the map from."

"But we didn't steal the map," Chinns stated.

Streak nodded. "Ah, so you'll take the treasure to the man the map was stolen from? Perhaps there will be a reward for it."

The brothers exchanged blank stares.

Streak smiled within. He had their thoughts tied up in

knots. The brothers weren't good men, but that didn't mean they didn't have good in them. Perhaps he could bring it out. After all, they were trying to be honest.

"There is a saying that goes 'To the conqueror go the spoils.' Do you agree?"

They nodded.

"You can try to kill me and take the treasure for yourself, or you can be my faithful servants for the next two years." He spread his wings for effect and added, "Or you can leave empty-handed and vow never to come back."

Chinns tried to speak in a sophisticated manner. "Er, may we confer?"

"You may, indeed."

The brothers turned their backs to him and spoke in a weird sort of orcen gibberish. Streak didn't really care what they were saying, but he was excited to hear the answer.

When the brothers turned around, they stood up.

Chinns said, "Um, we will serve you for two years, given we won't be asked to do anything foul."

Streak tilted his head and asked, "What do you mean?"

"We want a clean slate. No more robbing and stealing. We want to walk in an upright manner," Chinns said.

"Yeah, be respectable," Chubb added.

Streak reared his head back.

They cowered.

"No, I'm not going to attack you. I'm in shock. It seems the pair of you have had a change of heart."

"You saved our lives. We owe you that debt. And a wicked dragon wouldn't have done that. He'd have eaten us alive."

"Or turned us into pyres of flame," Chubb said and nodded. "We will be glad to serve you. For two years, unless a life debt is paid. We think those terms are fair."

Streak hadn't fully expected them to agree to his terms. A part of him still wanted the treasure for himself, even though he had absolutely no use for it. Another part of him needed to be entertained, but he still had to protect Grey Cloak and Dyphestive. He gave it some thought.

What am I going to do with these two nincompoops for the next two years?

"Let me ask you something. Have you ever heard of Zanna Paydark?"

They shook their heads.

Streak grinned. "Good. Because you're about to go through her training, and after this, you'll never forget the name."

40

CHINNS WALKED with Chubb on his shoulders. Both men carried buckets full of water in their outstretched arms. They navigated through the woodland at the base of the high hills with Streak trailing behind them.

"Don't spill a drop. If you do, we'll have to go back to the pond and start over again," Streak said.

Chinns groaned. "My legs and shoulders are killing me. When can we switch?"

"Top of the rise." Streak had been tormenting them for months, waking them up early and making them work into the night. He made them exercise and train, performing all of the grueling tasks that Zanna had put Grey Cloak and Dyphestive through. "Be strong. You're almost there."

"I'll die before I get there," Chinns said. He labored for breath as he chugged his way up the path.

"You can do it, brother. You're strong. Strong like a wild ox!" Chubb said. "Make that climb!"

The brothers encouraging one another was one of the qualities Streak enjoyed about them. If one pushed, the other pushed back harder. They had a lot of fight in them.

With the thick muscles knotted up in his back, Chinns fought his way to the top. His bare feet slipped a time or two, but he didn't spill a drop.

Over their training, the layers of fat on the orcen men had been shed and replaced by rock-hard muscle. The brawn rippled underneath their hairy shoulders and chests. Their stomachs were flat and lean. Chinns still carried more fat than his brother, and a second chin still hung under his jaw, but it was a lot less than the four rolls of neck fat he'd once had.

Chinns topped the climb.

Chubb raised his buckets of water and shouted at the sky, "Wahoo!"

"Well done." Streak joined them at the top. He caught them lowering their buckets and said, "Keep those arms up. This isn't over yet."

Chinns objected, "But, Master—"

"Quiet! Or you won't eat tonight!"

The brothers lifted the weighty buckets, their arms flexing. As they huffed and puffed, their faces turned bloodred.

Streak gave in. "Okay, you can drop them."

Chinns set down his buckets first, and Chubb handed

his down to him. Chubb started to stand on Chinns's shoulders and said, "Let's do it."

"I'll give you what I have." Chinns squatted down and thrust himself upward.

Chubb's powerful legs launched him into the air. Arms wide and legs pinned together, he floated in the sky, flipping backward and falling quietly to his feet. With one mitt in the ground, he said, "How was that, Master Streak?"

"You aren't going to win any gymnastics medals, but for a brute like you, not bad. Not bad at all," he said with a nod of approval. "Now, quench your thirst. You've done well. We'll cook venison tonight."

The brothers bumped forearms and grinned, showing mouthfuls of crooked yellow teeth.

"Master Streak," Chinns said, "will you tell us more stories of the heroes of old tonight? We so enjoy them."

Streak nodded. "You've put forth a worthy effort. I'll be happy to oblige."

With the moon rising over the plains, they resumed their trek up the hill.

"I like the tales about the other world. The one with horseless wagons and the faceless metal dragons," Chubb said with a dreamy expression. "And women so beautiful, delicate, and clean, with painted faces and... What did you call those outfits?"

"Bikinis," Streaks stated.

"Ah, yes, bi-kinis," Chubb continued, struggling to

pronounce it. "And the food. The popcorn and ice that tastes like cream." He licked his lips. "I want that."

Chubb spoke of the world Streak had visited for a spell. When he, Grey Cloak, and Dyphestive had dived into the Time Mural to escape the underlings, Streak made a side trip through part of the wormhole. He was stranded there for many weeks, long enough to embrace its colorful, vibrant, and advanced civilization.

Sometimes I miss that place. Definitely the food and entertainment. And Smoke, Sid, Sticks, and Boon, of course. Good times. Ah, good times for all. I wonder how they're doing.

Chinns shoved his brother. "We hear about the heroes tonight. Not the other world with people of one race. That's boring. I want to know more about the time of fire and dragons. The Sky Riders who ride on waves of clouds that bring the thunder."

"Pah, have it your way, brother." Chubb stretched, cracking his back. "I'll be glad to hear anything the master speaks."

Streak moseyed along behind them. In many ways, they were like children who'd never been properly reared or given education of any sort. They'd survived by doing only what they knew—looting and stealing. After a short time with Streak, they became like sponges, eager to learn and get better at everything. They were much older than he was, but he became like a parent or older brother to them. And they had no idea what his age was.

They reached the plateau in the mountains where the statues of Grey Cloak and Dyphestive waited. The life-size figurines were still covered in earthy growth and grit, but the camp had been cleared and the log cabin cleaned out.

Like a pair of obedient children, Chinns and Chubb started a campfire and filled the spit over the flame with deer meat. As the food cooked, they sat down with Grey Cloak and Dyphestive, as if they were part of the same company.

Chinns said, "Tell us more about the big man, Iron Bones. I like that one."

Streak nodded. "Have you ever heard of the Doom Riders?"

The brothers sat up and shook their heads.

Chinns replied, "No, but I like the sound of them."

CHAPTER 41—THE PRESENT: THE CHASM OF CHAOS

A COLD FEELING fell over Zora and clung to her for hours. The company had been traveling a network of paths that wound through the mountains, rising before sloping down again. The tunnels in the stark peaks bent around like giant-sized wormholes. The last wormhole was what had her worried. They hadn't seen daylight in hours, and she'd completely lost track of time.

West led the way, torch lifted in one hand and wood axe in the other. The strong-backed mountaineer moved like a ghost through the hills and tunnels, never stopping to rest and often mumbling.

Zora remained somewhere between the others. Razor and Gorva guarded the rear. Beak and Tatiana trailed on West's heels, with Tatiana using the Star of Light like a personal torch. Even with company, Zora felt alone. Her failure to master the dragon charm consumed her. In the past, she'd connected with stone and dragon without giving it so much as a thought. It felt as natural as speaking. But the ability seemed to be gone.

She caught Tatiana glancing back at her and acknowledged her with a nod.

Tatiana gave her a sympathetic look. Her eyes appeared tired, and the colorful luster of her tan skin had faded. Saving Razor had drained her more than she wanted to let on.

"West," Zora said, catching up to him.

He kept moving at a pace that she had to quick-step to catch up with.

"I think we need to rest."

He just kept moving.

She rushed up to him and hooked the back of his trousers with her hand. "West! Stop, please."

"Oh-ho," he said, shaking his head. "You'll have to forgive me. Once I start trekking, I don't stop until I get there."

"We know," she replied.

West set down his axe and lowered his pack to the ground. "I'm not used to traveling with others. I'm a lone wolf. Moving across the hills like I'm one of the wild. You see, you have to blend in, or you'll spook them, or they'll attack when scared or hungry."

The other party members took a seat on the gritty

cavern floor. Gorva and Razor shared a waterskin, and she offered it to the others.

"What happens if your torch goes out?" Gorva asked West.

"Ah-ha, funny you should ask. As a matter of fact, I've had that happen before. Talk about scary, being trapped in the pitch-black." West rubbed his knees. "The first time it happened to me, I was young and not wise, obviously. I wandered into a hole like this, got caught up in my exploration, then my torch died out. Talk about a cold sweat. I can feel it just talking about it." He reached into his pack, grabbed a strip of dried meat, and began eating while looking around absentmindedly.

Gorva leaned forward and asked, "Well, how did you get out?"

"Ah, yes, I suppose I should finish the story." West wiped his fingers on his shirt. "After a lot of moaning and crying, I recalled what my father taught me. Not to trust only one sense but to use them all." He flicked his ear. "I have these big ears like a rabbit. A nose like a hound and a gift for smelling and tasting things." He stretched out his fingers. "You might not know it, but there is a breeze in here. I can feel it. I can smell the cold coming through the outside. It made a path for me that day and let me back outside. I learned a lot about myself that day."

"What was that?" Razor asked.

"Always pack extra torches." West slapped his knee and chortled. "My senses may be good, but I prefer the light."

Gorva sat up, her nostrils flaring. "We're getting close, aren't we?"

West gave her a sideways look. "Aye. How did you know that?"

"I smell fire, like brimstone. I've smelled it for a while, but I thought it was my imagination."

"No, your senses tell you right. The Flaming Fence is near. That smell lets me know I'm still on the right course," he said. He winked at Zora. "After all, it has been a while. And these tunnels are like walking through a titan's intestines." He stood back up and grabbed his pack. "Enough rest. Let's go."

Zora's stomach fluttered. Since Gorva had mentioned it, she could have sworn she could feel the heat from the fence on her face. They were closing in on a place buried away from civilization for a reason—separated from an evil without redemption. She shivered.

Tatiana helped Zora to her feet. She looked deep into her eyes and said, "We can do this."

"I know. We have to."

The deeper they went, the more expansive the cavern became. The high ceiling swallowed their light with darkness, and they could only see a few dozen yards away.

West came to a natural stone bridge that crossed over a chasm and said, "Careful, now. The bridge is wide, but I wouldn't stand close to the edges." He started across. "It's slick."

Tatiana stood at the bridge's edge. She closed her eyes, and the Star of Light burned brighter, illuminating the cavern in daylight.

Down inside the chasm were more bridges crossing over level by level, going deeper into the earth.

"Whoa," Razor said. "That's a lot of bridges. How much deeper does it go?"

West held his torch over the bridge and said, "There's seven of them. This is the first. It's not too late to turn back. It makes no difference to me. No one is going to invade the peaks, no matter who's in charge. It's difficult living."

Zora took a deep breath and asked, "Is everyone still on board?"

The company nodded.

She followed West. Her fingers dug into her palm, and she tingled all over.

How did I ever get caught up in this?

42

THE TREK down into the mountain was steep but manage-
able. The tunnels at the end of the bridges bent in a downward slope to the next level, where the next bridge crossed
again.

A chilly breeze flowed through the chasm, rustling
their clothing and fanning the flames on the torches. The
lingering scent of brimstone strengthened.

Zora peered up. The distance between the levels of
bridges was huge, and the next one appeared to be farther
away than the others that had faded away into the
darkness.

"Almost there," West said quietly. "The final bridge is
next."

Something about the way he said it sent tingles
crawling up her back. Zora had wanted to turn back the

previous day, but the point of no return had come. If her friends were willing to make the journey, she was too.

The tunnel leading away from the second-to-last bridge made a corkscrew twist to the bottom, and the final bridge, twice as long as the others, loomed before them. On the other side were two large stone gargoyles holding urns with fiery green flames.

"Are those skulls?" Beak asked. She'd been silent for the entire journey, as if the suffocating gloom had swallowed her tongue. "Oh my. They *are* skulls."

The bridge was made of skulls and skeleton bones of all shapes and sizes. They were from all of the races—men, orcs, elves, and even giants.

"I've never seen so many bones before in all of my days," Razor said with his hands gripping his hip swords. "How did they die?"

"Perhaps they're the bodies of those on the other side of the Flaming Fence," Tatiana said. Her jaw tightened. "Or this is from another depraved civilization from a forgotten age."

"It's sick. That's what it is," Razor said. He turned to West. "Is it safe to cross?"

"As solid as rock. Quite a marvel, though I had my doubts the first time I crossed it." He nodded toward the other side. "Shall we? Oh, and don't look down. It's spooky."

They followed him with uncertainty written on their faces.

Zora's eyes were drawn toward her feet. Tormented skull faces appeared where they stepped and vanished when they walked away. The faces were angry and screaming.

Zora held one's gaze too long. Her legs locked up. A tortured woman's scream entered her head.

"Turn back! Don't be a fool! Turn back!" Snakes crawled out of the skull's mouth and eyes. She howled. "Turn back!"

Zora's knees buckled, and she teetered.

West wrapped his arm around her waist, and she shrieked.

He whisked her across the bridge and said, "I told you not to look down. Those haunted bones will spook you. They aren't much for conversation."

On the other side of the bridge, standing in the light of the towering urn-carrying gargoyles, the members of the party rubbed their eyes and heads.

"Anvils. I felt like my spirit was crawling out of me," Razor said. He held his hand before his eyes. His usually steady fingers trembled. "That's not the worst of it, is it?"

West shrugged. "I can only imagine it worsens on the other side of that door." He pointed inside the deep alcove that lay between the gargoyle statues. The cavern was outlined in shelves of skulls resting on bones, with the largest at the bottom and smallest on the top.

Tatiana approached the ancient doorway. It rose several feet above her head and was outlined by runes that looked like flames. The doors were made of black wood with dull metal handles. She reached for the handles.

Zora grabbed her hand. "Are you sure that's wise? West, have you opened them before?"

He shook his head. "This is as far as I've come. This is as far as I go."

"This is what we're here for," Tatiana said.

Zora stared at the imposing doors. The chill in her bones grew colder. "Are you certain this is the only way?"

"Yes, this is what I saw in the Eye of the Sky Riders. This is the entrance to the Nether Realm. On the other side, the Flaming Fence lies where the Dragon Helm is held."

"Held?" Razor asked. "Held by whom?"

"It lies and waits. That's all that I know." Tatiana's long fingers danced inches away from the handles.

Zora's heart thumped, and she gulped. Tatiana's hands locked around the door handles.

The flaming runes crackled and started to glow, dimly at first then brighter, bathing the chamber of skulls in orange light.

Around the door's border, orange light crept through.

The chill air started to warm as the entrance doors heated.

Zora stepped back and licked the salty sweat from her

upper lip. The chamber felt like a furnace, and a roar of fire filled the room. "Tatiana! Are you sure you want to do this?"

With her eyes fixed on the door, Tatiana tugged on the handles.

The doors flew open, hurtling her backward.

Razor and Gorva caught her in their arms and held her upright.

Expressions of astonishment hung on everyone's faces as they all looked through the doorway at the Flaming Fence standing several stories high.

"That's one big fire," West said. "I shudder to imagine what's kept on the other side of it."

43

THE FLAMING FENCE stretched from wall to wall and from floor to ceiling. Its fires cascaded up and downward like waterfalls. The air was hazy, and the ground had little holes that steamed.

One at a time, led by Tatiana, Talon made its way through the doorway.

Squinting and shielding his face with his arm, Razor said, "Pretty. But how are we supposed to get through those flames without being turned into ashes?"

"The Star of Light will protect us. I think," Tatiana replied.

"You think? Glad we came all this way without a sure-fire plan. No pun intended." Razor drew one of his swords. "Let's get on with it, then."

"You can put that away. It won't do you any good."

Everyone turned toward the voice, which had come from behind them.

The apparition of Dalsay stood in the doorway. The bookish wizard's hair was as long as the day he'd died. His features were sharp, and his intelligent, piercing eyes were as white as moonbeams. The hem of his blue wizard robes moved in waves above his sandaled feet. He wore a grim expression.

"Dalsay, my love," Tatiana said, rushing toward him. "Where have you been?"

He reached for her, but her hands passed through his. "My dearest, the battle with the underlings nearly stole my existence. It's taken a great deal of time to recover. I've been searching."

"And you've found us."

"Aye, I have." His ghostly hand brushed over Tatiana's cheek. "And you are as beautiful as ever. I've missed you."

"And I, you."

Dalsay's gaze turned serious. "I've come to warn you. This is a risky plan. Far more dangerous than you can imagine. If you cross over, there is no guarantee you can cross back. The fence is designed to keep the wicked and depraved within. Search your hearts. Be certain your intentions are true and honest. If they're not, you will be doomed."

"How can we know for sure?" Zora asked.

"Well, judging by your actions, I believe they are, but if

there is deceit among you, it will doom that person and possibly spell doom for you all," he said. Dalsay floated toward the wall of flame. "I never imagined it would come to this." He looked over his shoulder. "And you're certain the Dragon Helm resides on the other side?"

Tatiana nodded. "I am."

"I'd propose you test the wall. Cross over and return, but its power will drain you. The Star of Light will protect you but not for long. This is dangerous."

"I know the consequences, but I see no other way," Tatiana replied. "This is the only way to defeat Black Frost and his forces."

"We hope." Dalsay gazed at all of them. "Be warned. The vilest of all the races dwell on the other side. Liars, murderers, deceivers. They turned their backs on what was right and chose what is wrong. They take glee in torment and torture. But most of all, don't be fooled by their deceptions. They're as cunning as serpents and as ravenous as wolves. Don't lower your guard. Fetch the helm and don't look back."

Chill bumps broke out on Zora's arms. "Will you be joining us?"

"There is little I can do but watch over you. I don't want to reveal myself in case of trouble."

"Well, thanks for showing up. Maybe you and Mountain Man can use the time to get to know each other better. Play a few hands of Birds," Razor said as he stuffed his sword back into his sheath. "What good is a ghost, anyway?"

"Agreed," Gorva said. "Can you at least tell us what the horrors we can expect on the other side look like? Men? Beasts? Dragons?"

"The worst of all of those things."

"Big help," Razor said. "And you say our weapons won't do us any good."

"It never hurts to take them," Dalsay replied. "But the lost aren't looking for a fight. They're looking for a way out. They try to use you to get it."

"Perhaps I should go alone," Tatiana suggested.

"No, we're all in this together," Zora stated.

"It's your best chance to make it out alive," Dalsay agreed.

"No offense, but all of this talk is making me more uneasy," Beak said. "In the Honor Guard, we have a saying. 'Act before doubt takes you out.'"

"Sound advice to me." Razor stepped through Dalsay's ghost. "Tatiana, let's do this before your friendly ghost scares us out of it."

"Gather around." Tatiana lifted the Star of Light above their heads and started to recite her mantra. Her lips moved like butterflies' wings. A radiant dome of rosy energy appeared all around them. "Stay close. We're going in."

The closer they moved toward the Flaming Fence, the

more suffocating the air became. It was little different from the dragon flame that had almost consumed Zora and Tatiana days earlier. The air became as hot as an open oven. Every piece of clothing clung to Zora's sweaty body.

Waterfalls of fire loomed over them, growing ever higher the closer they came. Then they pushed into the wall, and the dome sizzled like a thousand pieces of bacon.

"Move quickly!" Tatiana urged them. "The flame is fierce!"

"You don't have to tell me twice. Go! Go!" Razor insisted.

Flame consumed them. Zora lost her bearings. The roar of the fire drowned out all other sounds. She grabbed Tatiana's free hand and held on like a child. She tried to yell at Tatiana, "Turn back!" but no sound could be heard.

Tatiana's eyes were sealed shut. She marched onward with her chin high and sweat rolling down her cheeks. Her legs fought for every step.

Zora glanced at her friends. Their faces were white with terror. Silent shouts came from their lips.

She shouted at Tatiana one last time. "Turn around, or we'll be cooked to death!"

44

A WHITE FLASH BLINDED ZORA, making her stumble and fall.

Tatiana's strong grip dragged her forward until her hand let go.

The sound of roaring flames faded away.

I'm going to die.

A blanket of cold air caressed Zora's body like a winter-morning breeze. She curled up, trembling. The fire had gone, replaced by the chill air of the depths.

Panting, Zora rubbed the dark spots from her eyes. She heard groaning. Once her vision cleared, she saw her company strewn across the ground, as disoriented as she was.

Tatiana was on her knees with her palms flat on the ground, dry heaving.

Sweat covered Razor's face like raindrops, and he brushed his damp hair from his eyes and gasped for air.

Gorva crawled to Beak, who lay on the ground, shivering like a scared dog.

The Flaming Fence was several yards behind them, and the doorway where they'd entered was gone. An open field of stone lay before them. They were on the other side.

"Tatiana," Zora said softly. The blood still rushed in her ears so loudly that she could barely hear herself talk. She tried to move toward her, but her legs were locked up. "Are you well?"

With a heavy sigh, Tatiana nodded. "That was worse than I imagined."

"You can say that again. I smelled my boots cooking," Razor said. Sweat dripped off of his chin, and he struggled to stand. He swayed. "Oh, I think I'm going to vomit."

Gorva scooted away. "Not on me."

He waved her off and took a couple of deep breaths of air. "I'm fine. Really thirsty but fine."

Using both hands, Gorva pulled Beak up by her arms. She embraced the shaking warrior. "You'll get your senses back. Give it a few moments."

"That's one return trip I'm not looking forward to." Beak wiped her face on her cloak. "Why are we doing this?"

"To save the world," Zora reminded her.

They stood inside another expansive cavern. The Flaming Fence exposed the upper limits of the ceiling, which was rich in stalactites. The ground was a field of stone that stretched as far as the eye could see.

"This isn't exactly what I had in mind," Razor said as he took a swig from his waterskin.

"And what did you have in mind?" Gorva asked.

"Something along the lines of hordes of the dead, like we met in Thannis." Razor tapped the handles of his swords. "Actually, worse than that."

"I'd plan on something worse, but we'll see." Tatiana stood. "Be wary and don't forget Dalsay's warnings. They are deceitful people down here. We're here to find the Dragon Helm and get out."

"The sooner, the better," Zora added as she rubbed her shoulders. "Let's go, shall we?"

She and Tatiana led the way. The trek was long, but there was only one way to go. At the far end of the cavern, another light source came up from the cavern floor.

Behind Tatiana, Razor, Gorva, and Beak walked together. Their gazes swept upward and from side to side as they anticipated a monstrous enemy that might drop down on them at any moment. But nothing came. The Nether Realm lay silent, aside from Talon's soft footfalls.

They closed in on the eerie light that crept out from the surface and bled over the stones.

Zora's skin prickled. A vast pit lay ahead, and she expected nothing less than throngs of a demonic enemy.

They all stooped as they approached. At the end of the

field, they came to a huge drop-off. Light flickered as they peered down upon a vast and magnificent city.

"Whoa," Razor said.

Zora blinked. At best, she'd expected to see a city in ruin, like Thannis, but perfectly crafted structures stood several stories tall. The roofs were flat with no smoking chimney stacks. Towers capped with jade and ruby quartz that twisted in the shape of flames overlooked the buildings. The streets were as wide as the breadth of several wagons.

People great and small wandered the roadways. Giants stood among men and small creatures with bat-like wings.

Razor sniffed. "I smell food. Something's cooking, and it's not us this time."

Zora smelled it, too, a delicious aroma like a hearty bowl of venison stew. Her tummy rumbled.

Tatiana pointed at a grand stone staircase that led down into the city. "Interesting. I don't see any sort of sentries." She started toward the steps.

"We're going to go down there?" Zora asked. "What are we supposed to do once we see them? Ask them where the Dragon Helm is?"

Tatiana raised her eyebrows. "Of course not, and pardon me for being hasty." She held out her hand. "May I have a dragon charm? I'll need it to locate the helm."

Zora opened her satchel and handed a charm over.

"Hang on to it. I have two more, not that they're doing me any good."

Tatiana clutched the dragon charm and closed her eyes. Her lips twitched. The charm pulsed with light then dimmed. She nodded and said, "The Dragon Helm awaits down there. The charm will guide us to it." As she started down the staircase, she looked back up at her comrades. "The people of the Nether Realm won't suspect anything if we don't do anything suspicious. They don't get many visitors. Hence, they don't expect any."

"What's that supposed to mean?" Razor asked.

"Simple," Tatiana answered. "Act like you belong."

45

Twenty flights of stairs later, Talon reached the land of the underworld city. The first thing Zora noticed was another Flaming Fence high above the city, casting light like the sun.

"Will you look at that," Razor said. "A sky made of fire. We're doomed, aren't we?"

Surrounding the strange city was a countryside. Stone cottages were scattered all over the sprawling land. Men and women sat huddled in their front-porch chairs, and farmers worked in fields with hoes. Strange deerlike creatures drank from small pools and lakes. The scene was an imitation of life in the world above but darker and different.

Talon strolled into the city like it was an ordinary day. Merchants hustled after customers who walked by. Giant men, over nine feet tall, made conversations with those that were much smaller.

The buildings were made from a stark-black but beautiful stone. Each and every block was tightly fitted together. The doorways had no doors, and the windows had no shutters.

Many people—men, women, dwarves, elves, and orcs—greeted the party as they walked by, treating them no different from one another. All of them had pink skin, not bodies of rotting and broken flesh as Talon had expected.

The streets went on as far as the eye could see. Seas of people walked in harmony. Men and women strolled arm in arm. Others sang, whistled, and danced.

"This is not what I expected at all," Gorva said as she stopped at a gorgeous fountain spitting out the purest of waters from the mouths of golden fish. "These people seem happy."

Zora agreed. She avoid the people's eyes as best she could but studied their clothing and movements. Their garb was woven from warm-colored and comfortable fabrics. Many wore sandals, while others wore shiny leather boots. Intoxicating perfumes wafted from the beautiful women who strolled by in sultry clothing, batting their eyelashes.

The men were durable, well-framed, easygoing, and polite. They shook hands with one another, squeezed shoulders, and tossed their heads back with robust laughter. The world was illuminated compared to the one that had darkened above. The people were all smiles. The sun, so to speak, always shone.

Two orcen cooks were smoking a large boar over a pit of fire. Juices dripped from the beast and sizzled in the flames.

"I don't know about all of you, but I could stand to eat something." Razor scanned the building. "And it wouldn't surprise me a bit if they made great ale here. This place appears to have everything." He wandered closer to the firepit and stood near the orcs. "Hello, fellas."

They returned quick nods.

"Smells good."

Gorva tugged him along by the collar. "I'll feed you later. Come along."

"But it smells so good."

"I wouldn't mind getting something to eat myself. I'm starving," Zora said. Everything that surrounded her seemed to whet her appetite.

In addition to the food stalls, clothing and pottery shops lined the streets. Jewelry was displayed behind plate glass windows. Men marched through the streets playing horns and banging on drums with their shoulders rocking to the beat. Talon found celebrations of one sort or another on every other corner. The streets were half-filled with jubilation.

"It was never this nice in Gapoli," Zora said.

Tatiana snapped her fingers in front of Zora's face.

"Remember why we're here. Don't let their temptations draw you in."

Everywhere Zora looked, handsome men tipped their caps, winked, or grinned. She blushed a time or two and nearly melted when a dark-eyed elf brought her a bouquet of roses and wished her well.

Talon covered many blocks, passing thousands of people. The Under Realm didn't appear to end. And above them, the Flaming Fence flickered, like one endless ceiling.

Razor strolled along with an easy gait, taking it all in and nodding. Beak moseyed about with the same dreamy expression. But Gorva's somber demeanor hadn't changed at all.

Zora's feet were sore, and her legs were tired, but she matched Tatiana's long, steady stride. She spotted children of all the races playing in fountains of crystal-clear water. Her thoughts lingered on marriage and having offspring of her own. Among the youths splashing and playing in the waters, she thought she saw herself and Bowbreaker standing together. She was holding a baby and smiling. But when she blinked, the image was gone.

A rotund little man wearing a gold shirt and a lavender vest ran up to them, beckoning them with his chubby little fingers. "Come. Come," he said to them. "I have the best food. I have the best drink. Whet your appetites at Zondar's Den of Delights." He raised his furry eyebrows at Razor and pointed at his tavern, where women danced and blew kisses on the stoop. "Many delights."

Razor's mouth gaped.

Gorva closed it back, pushed Zondar aside, and said, "He's not hungry for anything."

"Yes, I am," Razor objected with his eyes fixed on the women.

"No, you're not." Gorva towed him along by the wrist and caught up with Tatiana. "We need to find this helm fast. Are we close?"

"I believe so. The sensation in the dragon charm is getting stronger."

A trio of handsome orcen warriors caught Gorva's eye. They were tan and had long locks of waxen black hair and arms full of muscles. They showed their teeth at her, and one of them gave her a wink.

Gorva swallowed the lump in her throat and said, "Tatiana, wherever we're going, we need to get there quickly."

46

TATIANA CAME to a stop at the bottom of a staircase leading up to a tremendous palace made of stone. "The Dragon Helm lies in there," she said.

The palace was nothing like Zora had ever seen. The building was probably one hundred yards wide. The stairs ran all the way across the front and had several levels. Pillars of giant men made of stone held the eaves of the grand building up. Massive urns burned at the top of the stairs. The flames were green and quavering.

On top of the very center of the building was a huge dome that towered over everything. A spire and a dragon sculpture made of dark metal perched on the top. Its scales glinted, catching the light from the burning sky.

Zora had been to Dark Mountain and moved through its foreboding passes, but she'd never seen or imagined such a structure. "Are we really going to walk straight in there? Shouldn't we be more subtle?"

"I don't see any cause for alarm," Tatiana said. "No one here pays our presence any more mind than anyone else has so far. But we don't want to talk and make friends. The more of these people we avoid, the better, but don't be offensive and draw attention."

A group of elves came down the stairs. They wore flowing robes made of fine silk and casually waved as they passed.

"Obviously, someone lives here, don't they?" Beak asked.

Tatiana shrugged. "No doubt there is some form of government. But it is difficult to say without asking questions, which we won't be doing." She started up the stairs.

"Sounds good to me," Razor said. He took two steps at a time. "What's a little more walking gonna hurt? After all, my boots barely feel like they're on fire."

Beak fell in step behind him.

Zora hung back with Gorva. "How do you feel about this place?"

"I don't know what to make of it. Everything is pleasant. It's not what I expected. Look at me. I carry a spear, and no one asks any questions," Gorva said.

"We all have weapons, and many of them do too," Zora replied as she scanned the crowds behind them. "If they're so peaceful, why would they need weapons?" She started up the stairs with Gorva.

"I think they're in a dreamlike state. Well, either they are, or we are. I don't see, smell, or hear anything wrong, but every hair on my neck is standing on end," Gorva admitted. "When the time comes to fight, I'll be ready."

"Agreed. This place is like Thannis but different. I fully expect the enemy to climb out of the walls at any moment." Zora followed the others until they reached the top.

The giants sculpted into pillars stood twenty feet tall. They guarded the palace's entrance, and their downcast eyes seemed to follow the company's every move.

Another short flight of stairs led into the palace's grand entrance. A huge set of steel doors was wide open, revealing a rotunda. The floors and walls were polished white stone with black-and-gray marbling. Flecks of gold and streams of silver rested within the majestic rock. The dome loomed high above them. Several balconies ran along its inner ring, and people stood upon them, gazing down.

Zora marveled at their surroundings. She'd never been in a room so large before. The people walking the floor were little more than ants, and even the giant people appeared small. In a building so vast, the Dragon Helm could be anywhere.

Tatiana moved forward with steady determination, eyes forward and jaw muscles clenching.

Hallways led out of the rotunda to the right, left, and forward. Talon moved into the one that led them toward the back of the building. Beautiful paintings in frames trimmed in gold hung on the walls. The people in the huge paintings were so realistic that Zora felt she could walk into them. The eyes in the paintings seemed to follow them everywhere they went. Zora couldn't shake that feeling.

Between the paintings were open doors to other chambers. Men were gathered within, discussing the affairs of the Nether Realm like statesmen.

"All of this walking is getting old, Tatiana," Razor said. He moved awkwardly. "My buttocks are tightening up."

"I believe we're almost there," Tatiana replied. She kept walking straight down the hall.

At the far end, another rotunda waited. It was smaller than, but otherwise identical to, the one at the entrance.

Tatiana stopped just inside the rotunda with her gaze fixed on the object in the center of the room. A grandiose pedestal made of gold held an open-faced warrior's helmet covered in brilliant gemstones that twinkled like stars.

"Is that it?" Razor asked.

"It is," Tatiana answered.

"Well, let's snatch it while no one's looking." He started into the room.

Gorva grabbed him. "Be patient. Do you really think they'd leave something as precious as that unguarded?"

"It looks to me like they aren't guarding anything," he replied.

A handful of people were passing through the rotunda. Some of them took a moment to stop and admire the Dragon Helm, though it wasn't the only special object in the room. Along the walls were display cases filled with other objects, such as statues of people wearing showy clothing and finely crafted armor.

Zora nodded. "Come on. Since we've come all this way, let's get a closer look at it."

47

THE PRECIOUS STONES in the Dragon Helm varied in shape, size, and color. Smaller stones outlined the rim and the face. Larger stones formed rows from front to back, straight down the middle, and on the sides. Hundreds of larger and smaller stones filled in everywhere else.

"All of those are dragon charms?" Razor rubbed his jaw. "That helm must be worth a fortune. Are you sure it controls dragons? Because, you know, we could live pretty well off it."

"This is it. This is the Helm of Dragons that the Wizard Watch constructed to battle Black Frost. It is all that we have gathered." Tatiana glanced at Zora. "Almost all."

"Who's going to use it?" Beak asked.

"It will take a special person to control it. Most likely a natural," Tatiana replied. "We can't say for sure. The helm was created with a special purpose in mind—to control Black Frost and other dragons—but it has yet to be tested."

"What if Black Frost makes his own Dragon Helm?" Razor asked.

They gave him defeated looks.

He shrugged. "Shouldn't we plan for everything?"

"Razor is right," Tatiana said. "And the Wizard Watch thought this through. There is no evidence that Black Frost uses his charms other than to equip more dragon riders. Hence, his strategy is different and effective, while our strategy is... well, more desperate."

"Are you telling me we came all this way for something that might not work?" Razor asked. "I almost got eaten by a frog, for dragons' sake."

Gorva chuckled.

"What are you laughing at?"

"It would have been a disgraceful way to go. But I would have lied about your demise to preserve your precious reputation."

He shook his head. "Well, thanks."

"So, what do we do now? Take it?" Zora asked.

A giant approached. He stood nearly eight feet tall and had a lean build, pale skin, dark rings around his eyes, and a clean-shaven head. He wore long robes the color of a gray sky. He stood behind them with his hands behind his back, admiring the helm. "It's beautiful," he said in a rich, resonant voice. "Isn't it?"

Razor looked back over his shoulder and said, "Uh, yes, very much so."

The giant man nodded. "We knew you would come for it," he stated. "That is why we made it easy to find."

"Excuse me?" Razor asked as his hands found his swords' handles.

Zora turned toward the giant, moved in front of Razor, and asked, "What are you talking about?"

"There is no need to be concerned, little ones. I am not here to harm you or sound the alarm. The Nether Realm welcomes you. I am Utlas, speaker of the Realm."

No one said a word for several moments. Utlas's eyes remained fixed on the Dragon Helm.

Zora's tongue stuck to the roof of her mouth. Utlas's words shocked her. They'd waltzed into the Nether Realm with a false sense of security, but they'd been spied on from the beginning. She summoned her courage and asked, "What is it you want, Utlas?"

"It's not what I want. It's what we all want. A fair exchange. You want the Dragon Helm, and you can have it, for a price."

Razor rolled his eyes. "Of course. I should have known we couldn't take it away without paying. So what do you want—"

Gorva clamped her hand over his mouth.

"What did you have in mind?" Zora asked.

"Please, come with me. And don't worry. The Dragon

Helm won't be going anywhere." Utlas bowed politely to all of them and added, "Please, follow."

As Utlas led them toward the back of the palace, Talon exchanged uneasy glances but followed the giant's long, slow strides.

"I'm sure you're familiar with our history," Utlas said with his giant fingers still clasped behind his back. "The Time of Troubles was our folly. Our greed and lust for power consumed us. We've had centuries to dwell upon our mistakes. And I hope you can see we have learned the errors of our ways and over time have redeemed ourselves."

"No one can redeem themselves," Razor stated.

"Ah, but that's not true." Utlas exited the back of the palace. "Please, see more of what we have created."

A balcony with a stone railing overlooked the most breathtaking view Zora had ever seen. An endless lake of clear blue water sat a hundred feet below. Dragons with spectacularly colored scales soared across the sky. Rocks floated above the water with people riding on them, basking underneath the light of the Flaming Fence.

Beak leaned over the railing. "It's marvelous."

"As you can see, we have taken this hole that we were sent to rot in and fashioned it into a remarkable home for all," Utlas said with a pleasant smile. "This is the result of what happened when we took a deep look within ourselves. We found something good and brought it forth."

"My father said good doesn't come from within. It

comes from faith in something far greater than us," Razor commented.

Utlas waved a hand, and an empty stone floating above the water came toward them. He climbed on top of it. "Come. There is plenty of room for all."

Zora hesitated. "I like discussing matters right here. Tell us, Utlas, what do you have in mind?"

48

"I WON'T DELAY ANY LONGER," Utlas said. "After all, you've made a very long journey to come here. I'm sure you're weary and require rest. But we will discuss what we require."

"We're listening," Zora said.

"We want the Flaming Fence taken down."

Zora felt the blood run out of her body. "Excuse me? You want us to remove the Flaming Fence? We didn't create it. Why would we have any idea how to take it down?"

Utlas pointed at Tatiana and said, "This one does. She is of the Wizard Watch, is she not? They built it. They can destroy it."

"That lore is long forgotten. Destroyed, after it was built, so your kind can never come out. I fear this is the only life for you, Utlas. What you have created here, you will have to make the best of."

"I see." He withdrew his hand and clenched his fist. "We long for the open sky and the wind on our faces. Despite the beauty, this is still a dark place. We want out. You must find the way. I plead with you."

"Utlas, would you please give us a moment to speak privately?" Zora asked.

"Certainly. Take your time. We are, if anything, patient." Utlas climbed onto the stone and floated away over the crystal lake.

"Tatiana, is this even possible?"

"Of course it isn't. Even if it were, we wouldn't do it," she said.

"Why not?" Beak asked. "They aren't any different from anyone else, so far as I can see. They're nice."

"Agreed, but maybe a little too nice," Razor said. "As much as I like them, my skin is still crawling."

"What are we supposed to do? If we don't make a deal with Utlas, they won't let us leave with the Dragon Helm. We'll be trapped here," Gorva said.

"Not if we take it and run," Razor suggested.

"Why don't we tell him what he wants to hear, go get the Dragon Helm, and leave this place?" Zora said. "We only need to be convincing."

"You mean conniving," Tatiana replied. "That isn't how I like to negotiate. It always leads to bad things. And remember what Dalsay said. They're liars and deceivers. We need to figure out what we're really up against."

"What do you suggest?" Zora asked.

"Tell him no deal. Let's see what happens."

"Brilliant. Give him a swift kick in his giant nanoos, why don't you?" Razor rolled his eyes. "I don't think that will go well."

"He's coming back," Zora said. She looked at Razor. "I'll do the talking."

Utlas's slab of stone bumped against the balcony. "I hope you have come to a decision. Our people have been very eager since your arrival."

Zora fought to keep her voice from shaking. "Utlas, we can't help take down the Flaming Fence and free the Nether Realm. But there won't be a world for you to depart to if we don't save it. There won't be a Nether Realm either. Black Frost will destroy it. We understand if you won't part with the Dragon Helm. If we can't have it, we won't fight you. We will take our leave."

The stone-faced giant stood quietly for a moment. His long fingers rubbed his face. In a dark, resonant voice he said, "I see. You would play on our hopes and leave us stranded."

"No, we—"

"Silence, infidel invader!" Utlas pointed at her. "You will never leave." He beat his chest and lifted his voice to the sky. "We will never leave!" He glowered at all of them.

They each took a step back.

Utlas's eyes burned like torches, and his fingernails turned to flames. A fireball appeared in his hand, and he flung it toward the palace.

The flaming ball slammed into the palace walls with a thunderclap. The entire Nether Realm flickered. The porcelain walls of the palace began to crack and crumble, and the magnificent building transformed into rubble.

"What's going on here?" Razor pulled his sword. "This entire place is crumbling!"

"Gaze upon your future, fools!" Utlas said in a voice like the roar of water. Then he started to grow. "Look around you! See the lake that will be your home." He pointed behind him.

The crystal-clear water of the lake had turned into flaming lava. The people floating comfortably on the rocks suddenly floated in steel cages.

"That is your destiny! That is your doom!" Utlas had become at least twelve feet tall. "You don't want to make a deal with me." He placed his flaming fists on his hips. "Ha! I don't need a deal with you. I've already made a deal with Black Frost! That's why we've been waiting!"

"What?" Tatiana asked. "How?"

"Who cares how? We need to get out of here." Razor tugged on Tatiana's arm. "Come on!"

Beak drew her swords and said, "I think it's too late for any of us to go anywhere."

People filed out of the back of the palace.

"Oh my," Zora said.

The grand illusion that had fooled them all was gone. They weren't the same polished and polite people from before. Their skin was gray and ruddy, and their clothing was tattered. Their rusty armor rattled. All of their eyes were pitch-black, and their expressions were grim if not demonic. Numbering in the hundreds, they walled off the exit..

"We should have run for it when we had the chance," Razor said. "I knew this was a lousy plan. Utlas, we want another deal!"

"Ho ho, the little mortal says. It's too late for that, but I like your boldness." Utlas stepped down to the balcony. His rock had transformed into a floating cage for all of them.

The hordes of the lost crowded the party and stripped them of all of their goods. Forceful hands shoved Talon into the cage.

Gorva pushed back. "Easy!"

The horde locked them inside the cage. A lake of churning lava waited below.

Utlas peered down at them and said, "A shame you came all this way for nothing. But the Dragon Helm was the perfect bait. And now that I've captured you, I have orders to destroy it. But I'll let you dwell upon it." He pushed the floating cage away with his foot. "Oh, and the cage isn't locked. Feel free to climb out if you wish." He picked up Zora's satchel. "Interesting. What sort of treasures shall I find in here?" He picked up the Star of Light and Tatiana's dragon charm as well then waved. "Now, if you'll excuse me, I need to send a message to my dear friend Black Frost."

Talon pressed against the bars, staring down into the molten flames. They were beaten and broken.

No one had a word to say except Tatiana, who, with a defeated expression, said, "I'm sorry."

From a distance, Dalsay witnessed the demise of his companions. His ghostly state allowed him to pass through the Flaming Fence without harm and back again, where he joined West.

The mountaineer was sitting in the chamber with his back to the wall of skulls, sharpening his axe with a whetstone. He stood the moment he caught sight of Dalsay approaching. "What happened, ghost?"

"It's worse than I feared," Dalsay responded. He glided over and drifted down to where his feet touched the floor. "Black Frost is crafty and has set a trap. He made a deal with the Nether World. The only thing I can imagine is that he learned of the Dragon Helm from the underlings, Verbard and Catten. But that doesn't explain how he knew where it was."

"Perhaps there is a spy in your group."

Dalsay shook his head. "If that were the case, they wouldn't survive the wall of fire. No, there are many betrayers in the Wizard Watch that could have told him. Gossamer is one of them. I don't know, but it's possible that Black Frost located the Dragon Helm and hid it or let it lie in the Nether Realm to trap us."

"Sounds to me like the trap worked." West swung his axe onto his shoulder. "What do you want to do?"

"Find help. We need it."

CHAPTER 49—THE BLACK FOOTHILLS

TINISON RUBBED his hands over the campfire's flames and stared at the juice dripping off the body of a dead stag. He had a large bandage wrapped around his ribs, and he grimaced when he moved. "Oh, that's going to be good. Stag meat—there's nothing better. And there's enough to feed a family. Thank you, Anya and Cinder."

"Don't mention it," Cinder said. "But save a leg for me." The grand dragon lay in the woodland. His chin rested on the ground, and his bright eyes shone like giant fireflies in the night. His breath kept most of the area warm, and the snow had melted all around them.

Crane lay inside a small tent near the fire with his head peeked out. He gazed up through the pine branches at the stars. "They say that there are men who travel the stars. Have you ever heard that?"

Tinison picked off a piece of charred meat with his fingers. "Ah, hot!" He fanned them in the wind. "No, never heard of star travelers. Only Sky Riders." He put the food into his mouth. "Mmm, tender." While chewing, he said, "What do you think, Anya? You've flown high in the sky. Have you seen any star travelers?"

Anya stood at the edge of the camp, looking up at the Peaks. She'd spent the last two days and nights with the men in the small camp while searching the mountains from the skies. The gnawing in her gut hadn't ceased. It had eaten at her since she saw her friends vanish into the bowels of the Peaks of Ugrad.

"When I was a girl, my father told me stories about great ships that traveled between the stars, but I never believed him. He would tell me anything to get me to sleep," she said.

Crane rolled onto his belly. Wide-eyed, he said, "Really? Sometimes I dream I'm flying on a ship from star to star."

"No, you don't," she said.

Crane shrugged. "You're right. I was only making conversation."

Anya drew her sword. "Quiet," she whispered. "Someone comes."

"You have a good ear, milady!" West said heartily. The strapping woodsman left the cover of the trees and came into full view. "And I'm one to spook a snow leopard, but I wasn't really trying."

"Where are the others?" she asked.

Tinison jumped to his feet. "Tell me they aren't dead. Please tell me they aren't dead."

"They aren't dead, but they aren't living well either," West answered.

Dalsay appeared out of nowhere.

"What happened, wizard?" Anya demanded.

"They found the Dragon Helm," Dalsay answered, "but the minions of the Nether Realm were waiting. They are led by a giant man named Utlas. He has an alliance with Black Frost. It was a trap. I fear they saw us coming before we even started looking."

"What are you saying?" Anya wanted to grab the wizard by the collar and shake him. "They're trapped forever? Can't we get them out?"

"That's my hope, but we need a lot more help. Help that we don't have."

EPILOGUE: BATRAM'S BARTERY AND ARCANIA

ZANNA PAYDARK STOOD at the counter, eyeing a glass display case and pointing. "I want that. That. That and that."

Batram's cottony eyebrows wiggled. He was in halfling form, standing on the counter and wearing his red-and-white-striped coat with a yellow daisy in the front pocket. "That's going to be quite expensive."

"I know." She lifted a large leather sack, rose on tiptoe, and with a grunt set it on the counter. Gold coins and precious gemstones spilled out and rattled on the counter.

Batram's eyes gleamed. "That's quite a haul. My, oh my." He went over to the sack and stuck his head in the bag. "Where did you acquire all of this fortune? There are some very unique items in here."

"I've stayed busy the last decade."

He sat down on the edge of the counter and said, "You

know, Zanna, if you ever need anything, you don't have to pay me with treasure."

"I don't want to owe you anything, Batram. If anything, this is payback for all the help you've given over the years."

His eyes slid over the Cloak of Legends, and he whistled. "I'm curious. Where is your son? He didn't expire, did he?"

"No, he lives, so to speak."

Spiders crawled out of the nooks and crannies of the rafters by the hundreds. They made their way down the walls and scurred across the counter. Like worker ants, they filed into the sack, placed a coin or two on their backs, and hurried away in a steady train. Back up the walls they went, moved over to the shelves, and loaded the coins into different drawers.

Batram wrung his hands. "So, he doesn't need the cloak anymore?"

"Of course he does. I'm on my way to return it now. He's waiting."

"That's unfortunate." He reached for the garment. "I was always fond of the cloak."

Zanna started filling her pockets with the objects Batram had given her. "I need a Bandolier of Vials and the Eye of Enthrallment."

Batram sputtered. "Er, what Eye of Enthrallment do you mean?"

"You know the one. You traded Grey Cloak for it." She narrowed her eyes. "I need it."

"Er, well, I can provide the bandolier, but—" He scratched his wooly sideburns. "The eye, that will be more—"

"Don't dicker with me now, Batram. I've fought every troll in the Ten Valleys, slain giants in Monrath, and killed the Wasp King. That's only one chapter out of the book. You don't want to add another chapter, do you?"

"There's no need to be testy. We've always had a strong professional relationship. Don't spoil it now."

"This is it, Batram. The final battle is on."

He nodded. "I see." He stuck his fingers into his lower pocket and produced the Eye of Enthrallment. It was a perfect sapphire gemstone the size of a person's eye. "I hope you aren't going to do anything rash."

She took it. "I'll do what I must do."

The spiders had emptied the sack of treasure. The last of them vanished beyond the cobwebs in the high ceiling.

Zanna gathered the sack, and the Bandolier of Vials appeared on the counter. "It's been a pleasure doing business with you, Batram." She reached into her cloak pocket, fished out another small sack, and tossed it to him. "Those diamonds and pearls ought to hold you. Thanks for dealing honestly."

Batram waved and said, "Goodbye, Zanna. I hope to do business again."

"Don't count on it." She stepped on the boar's-head rug.

"Thanks for coming!" the boar said. "Hurry back!"

Zanna stood at the base of the hills where she'd abandoned her son in a body of stone the better part of a decade ago. With her cloak drawn about her shoulders, she started her climb in the shadows of the moonlight.

He's going to be furious with me. But I did what must be done. It was the only way to keep the realm safe.

She'd wrestled with her deception for years, carrying the burden of guilt on her shoulders.

I lied to my son. Dyphestive and Streak. They'll hate me, but they'll have to get over it.

On cat feet, Zanna crept up the last shelf of rock where her former plateau home waited. The crackle of a campfire caught her ear. The warm glow of flames could be seen casting shadows on the hilltop.

What's happening?

Zanna prowled through the trees to get a better vantage point. She spied a pair of burly men with shaggy hair in heavy coats huddled over the flames of an open fire. The statues of Grey Cloak and Dyphestive were gone.

No! What have these invaders done with them? Where is Streak?

Sword in hand, she crept into camp and snuck up

behind the men. She pushed the tip of her sword against one man's back and said, "Make any sudden moves, and I'll skewer your heart and roast it on those flames. Let me see your hands. Both of you."

The men lifted their arms.

The second man started, "Listen, this is a—"

"Silence!" She pushed her sword harder into the man's back. "In the blink of an eye, I swear I'll end both of you. Where are the statues?"

"What statues?" the second man asked.

Zanna banged the flat of her sword on the man's head.

"Ow!" He rubbed his head. "How'd you move that fast?"

She hit him in the head again then whacked the other one. "Silence!"

"Anvils! Will you stop doing that? Streak said you were mean, but—"

Zanna whacked them both in the heads again and said, "Stop speaking, both of you. Where is Streak?"

"I'm right here, Zanna," he called from the woodland. "And lay off my friends, will ya?"

She focused on the dragon coming down the high path in the darkness. "Who are they?"

"Meet Chinns and Chubb. Acolytes of mine."

Chubb said, "Nice to meet you, Master Paydark, though a bit unpleasant. What should we do, Master Streak?"

Zanna sheathed her blade. "Streak, what are you doing? Why are they calling you and me Master?"

Streak came into full view. "Unlike you, they're polite and well trained and do as I say."

Zanna eyed him. "I see you've grown considerably."

"There hasn't been much to do but grow." Streak stood between the height of a middling and a grand. "And wait for you to come back. I thought I'd be glad to see you, but now that you're here, I'm not so sure."

"I told you I would be back. Here I am."

"It's been over twenty seasons. What have you been doing all this time? Knitting a giant's quilt?"

"No, I've been getting ready for the next step in our journey. Where are they, Streak?"

Streak got nose to nose with Zanna, narrowed his eyes, and said, "Over the years, I've done a lot of thinking. So I put them somewhere safe." He pushed her back with his nose. "Somewhere safe from you."

Will Zanna and Streak battle it out?

How will Talon escape the clutches of the Nether Realm?

Is there a traitor among them?

Find out in The Flaming Fence: Dragon Wars - Book 17! On sale now!

Please, don't forget to leave a review of Bedlam: Dragon Wars - Book 16

ABOUT THE AUTHOR

*Check me out on Bookbub and follow: HalloranOn-BookBub

*I'd love it if you would subscribe to my mailing list: www.craighalloran.com

*On Facebook, you can find me at The Darkslayer Report or Craig Halloran.

*Twitter, Twitter, Twitter. I am there, too: www.twitter.com/CraigHalloran

*And of course, you can always email me at craig@thedarkslayer.com

See my book lists below!

OTHER BOOKS

Craig Halloran resides with his family outside his hometown of Charleston, West Virginia. When he isn't entertaining mankind, he is seeking adventure, working out, or watching sports. To learn more about him, go to www.thedarkslayer.com.

Check out all my great stories...

Free Books
> **The Red Citadel and the Sorcerer's Power**
> The Darkslayer: Brutal Beginnings
> Nath Dragon—Quest for the Thunderstone

The Chronicles of Dragon Series 1 (10-book series)
> The Hero, the Sword and the Dragons (Book 1)

Dragon Bones and Tombstones (Book 2)

Terror at the Temple (Book 3)

Clutch of the Cleric (Book 4)

Hunt for the Hero (Book 5)

Siege at the Settlements (Book 6)

Strife in the Sky (Book 7)

Fight and the Fury (Book 8)

War in the Winds (Book 9)

Finale (Book 10)

Boxset 1-5

Boxset 6-10

Collector's Edition 1-10

Tail of the Dragon, The Chronicles of Dragon, Series 2 (10-book series)

Tail of the Dragon #1

Claws of the Dragon #2

Battle of the Dragon #3

Eyes of the Dragon #4

Flight of the Dragon #5

Trial of the Dragon #6

Judgement of the Dragon #7

Wrath of the Dragon #8

Power of the Dragon #9

Hour of the Dragon #10

Boxset 1-5

Boxset 6-10

Collector's Edition 1-10

The Odyssey of Nath Dragon Series (New Series) (Prequel to Chronicles of Dragon)

Exiled

Enslaved

Deadly

Hunted

Strife

The Darkslayer Series 1 (6-book series)

Wrath of the Royals (Book 1)

Blades in the Night (Book 2)

Underling Revenge (Book 3)

Danger and the Druid (Book 4)

Outrage in the Outlands (Book 5)

Chaos at the Castle (Book 6)

Boxset 1-3

Boxset 4-6

Omnibus 1-6

The Darkslayer: Bish and Bone, Series 2 (10-book series)

Bish and Bone (Book 1)

Black Blood (Book 2)

Red Death (Book 3)

Lethal Liaisons (Book 4)

Torment and Terror (Book 5)

Brigands and Badlands (Book 6)

War in the Wasteland (Book 7)

Slaughter in the Streets (Book 8)

Hunt of the Beast (Book 9)

The Battle for Bone (Book 10)

Boxset 1-5

Boxset 6-10

Bish and Bone Omnibus (Books 1-10)

CLASH OF HEROES: Nath Dragon meets The Dark-slayer mini series

Book 1

Book 2

Book 3

The Henchmen Chronicles

The King's Henchmen

The King's Assassin

The King's Prisoner

The King's Conjurer

The King's Enemies

The King's Spies

The Gamma Earth Cycle

Escape from the Dominion

Flight from the Dominion

Prison of the Dominion

The Supernatural Bounty Hunter Files (10-book series)

Smoke Rising: Book 1

I Smell Smoke: Book 2

Where There's Smoke: Book 3

Smoke on the Water: Book 4

Smoke and Mirrors: Book 5

Up in Smoke: Book 6

Smoke Signals: Book 7

Holy Smoke: Book 8

Smoke Happens: Book 9

Smoke Out: Book 10

Boxset 1-5

Boxset 6-10

Collector's Edition 1-10

Zombie Impact Series

Zombie Day Care: Book 1

Zombie Rehab: Book 2

Zombie Warfare: Book 3

Boxset: Books 1-3

OTHER WORKS & NOVELLAS

The Red Citadel and the Sorcerer's Power

Made in the USA
Monee, IL
09 July 2021